THE
MAN WHO
HUNTS DEATH

Also by Michael Doyle

JAMES'S RAGTAG ADVENTURES IN QUESTWORLD
(LIGHT NOVELS)

Vol. 1: Return of the Goblin Queen
Vol. 2: The eye of the Earth
Vol 3: Trials of the Minotaur
Vol. 4: The Missing King
Vol. 5: Rise of the God King
Vol. 6: The Unchained Isle

ANTOINETTE: MONSTER VET
(MIDDLE-GRADE)

The Gnomatic Plague

BRIELLE'S MAGICAL ADVENTURES
(PICTURE BOOKS)

Brielle and the Tangled Mermaid
Brielle and the Clumsy Dragon

THE MAN WHO HUNTS DEATH

BRIE
HOUSE

This book is dedicated to my Grandma.

*Always pushing me to finish
my stories. Wish you were here
to read them all.*

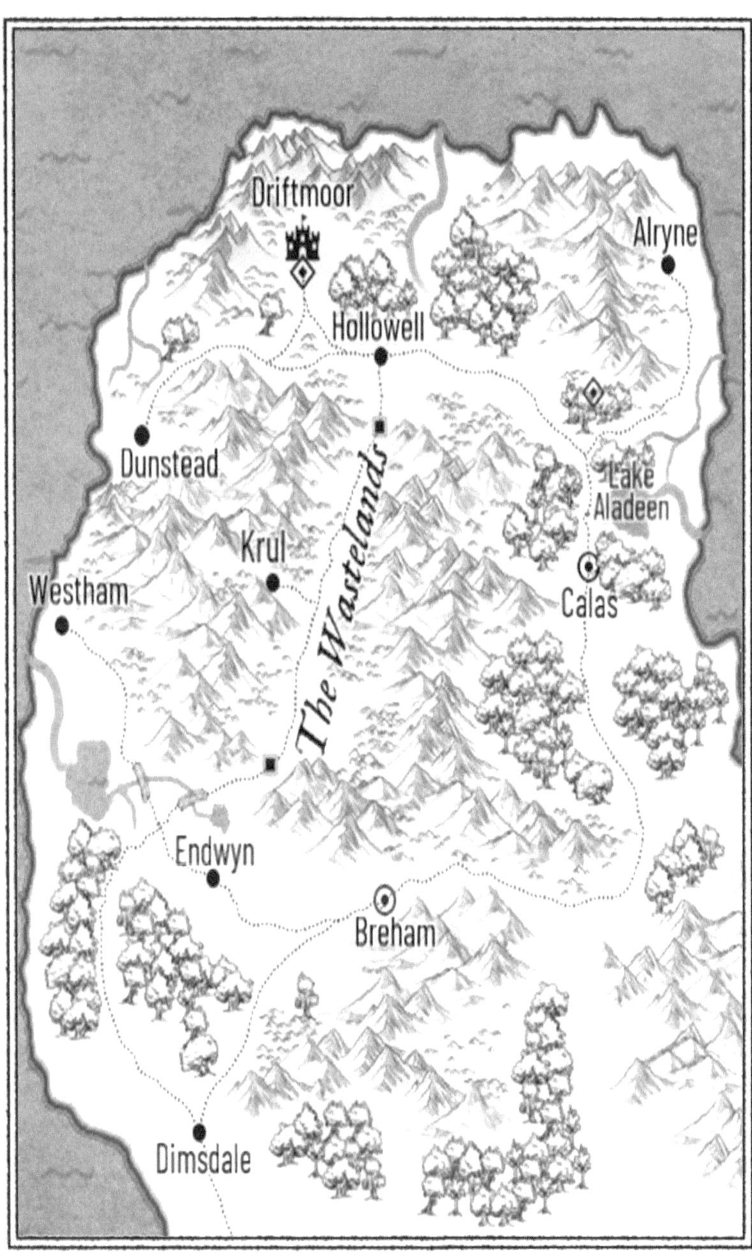

Driftmoor
Alryne
Hollowell
Dunstead
Lake
Aladeen
Krul
Calas
Westham
The Wastelands
Endwyn
Breham
Dimsdale

GUNVALD

CHAPTER ONE
BREHAM CITY SLUMS

Gunvald loathed Breham. From the pompous, self-important assholes in the Central City to the abhorrent slums that encircled it like a ring of filth, the place was a cesspit, so of course it was where Darius got himself locked up.

The foul breeze that swept through the slums brought with it the damp smell of shit, piss, and decay. It was a smell that stuck in Gunvald's nose and would undoubtedly stick there long after he left. While all of Breham's slums were vile shitholes, the eastern slums were exceptional in their squalor. Dilapidated buildings leaned precariously against crumbling walls.

Windows were shattered or boarded up. The debris littered street seemed to rot beneath his feet as he walked, while grime covered everything else around him. All of it creating an inescapable maze of feculence, especially in the dim moonlight.

Despite all that, Gunvald walked slowly and deliberately, his four swords, Dimittis, Iudicium, Cinis, and Obitus, leaving a thin line in the filthy street as they dragged on the ground.

A gift from Death herself, each sword was equipped with a thick ebony chain that wrapped itself around Gunvald's torso, digging barbed hooks into flesh to hold them in place. It was purely out of spite that Gunvald let them drag behind him.

He didn't want to be in this place any longer than he had to, but if he had to storm a damn prison, he might as well have an ale or two in him beforehand, and he sure as shit wasn't gonna get one in Central City. All those nobles jerking each other off, convincing themselves that they're the elite capital of the world? Fuck that. He'd rather throw himself into prison right next to that idiot Darius.

By the time Gunvald turned down the alley toward The Wretched Dove, the wind had picked up considerably and blew his ragged cloak over his right shoulder, exposing his ornate black cuirass. Even in the dim light of the moon, anybody with eyes could see that it was too rich for anyone in the slums to ever hope to afford, and shit like that always drew the wrong kind of attention.

"You take a wrong turn, Centi?" a man said, leaning against the cracked stone of the tavern wall, arms folded across his chest.

He was dressed in a ragged brown shirt and sported a long, unkempt, graying beard. Your typical slum dweller. With two similarly ugly men standing next to him, each holding wooden mugs.

One of the other men, a skinny, balding man, tapped his friend on the chest and said, "Well now, what do we have here?"

The three men fixed Gunvald with glassy-eyed gazes. "You lost or somethin', Centi." the third, a short, fat slob of a man, slurred.

Centi. A slum word used to describe people from the Central City. Gunvald never particularly cared for it. Not because of the negative connotation, but because it was lazy as shit. Uncreative. Even for a slum dweller with a gutter education.

"I'm just looking for a drink," Gunvald told them.

"A drink?" Graybeard chuckled.

"Then you've come to the right place," the balding man said, tossing his wooden mug.

The mug bounced off Gunvald's chest and clattered to the ground, its remnants dripping down the front of his cuirass.

Gunvald sighed. He had stolen the armor from a dead nobleman years ago, so it held no real sentimental value, but that made it no less aggravating that it was now covered in ale, and the three men's drunken laughter snapped Gunvald's last thread of patience.

Gunvald reached over his right shoulder, and the thick black chain connected to Cinis, the hand-and-a-half bastard sword, slithered into his grip like a steel serpent coiling around it's prey. The icy feeling that coursed through his hand was something he never got used to.

Gunvald swung Cinis by its chain in a wide arc over his head, driving the blade halfway through the top of the bald man's head with a loud crack and a splash of gore. The man's body jerked and convulsed, spraying a bloody mural on the tavern wall as he crumpled to the ground. Graybeard gaped at Gunvald, then down at his friend.

Gunvald wrenched back on the chain, pulling

the bloody sword from the man's skull. Cinis skittered across the ground as Gunvald held his other hand at his hip and let the longsword Dimittis find his grip.

He raised its thin steel blade over his head. Graybeard's eyes widened, and he flailed his arms up. Gunvald swung Dimittis down, cutting cleanly through the man's forearms.

Graybeard fell to his knees screaming as blood streamed from his stumps. Gunvald kicked the man over and turned his attention to the fat man.

The man's mouth moved rapidly, but no words came out. Piss blotted the crotch of his trousers. Gunvald dropped Dimittis to the ground, and the black chain of Iudicium coiled around his torso and down his arm, pulling the sword's hilt into his hand.

The fat man stumbled toward the street, a spattering of broken words streaming from his lips. Gunvald drew his arm back and hurled Iudicium at him. The hooked blade plunged into the man's back and burst from his chest, a large chunk of meat hanging off the tip. The man staggered forward. His screaming being the first coherent sound to leave his mouth since this whole thing started.

Gunvald pulled back the black chain, feeling the resistance of the hooked blade as it severed the man's spine. Gunvald stared at the fat slob for a second before flinging the sword and heavy chain over his shoulder and turning toward the peeling, rotting door of the Wretched Dove. He heard a man yelling obscenities from inside the tavern, and he sighed. It was the voice of the one man he was desperately hoping to avoid.

Gunvald grunted, "Get off," and tried to loosen the swords' chains from around his torso. In blatant defiance of his command, they coiled tighter.

"I said get off!" He clenched the chains and tried to pull them away from his chest.

There was a momentary battle of wills, but the chains finally relented and coiled back into their pommels. Gunvald growled, spat on the swords behind him, and then slammed open the tavern door.

The place was worse than he remembered. Its interior was a chaotic jumble of tables and chairs of every conceivable shape and size that looked like old driftwood randomly nailed together, and the air was heavy with the sour stench of stale ale and half-rotten food.

The bar—a ramshackle counter of decaying wooden doors balanced on equally decaying wooden barrels—was still standing on the far side of the room. The stools in front of it looked one fat ass away from collapsing.

Gunvald made his way towards the bar, and the handful of patrons went silent, except for the high constable, Olin Tibout.

"What the fuck, Gunvald?!" Olin shouted across the tavern, flailing his thick arms. His brow was deeply furrowed, and his large hands clenched into fists. He marched towards Gunvald, shoving aside a chair.

Despite being shorter than Gunvald, Olin's bulging muscles gave him the illusion of being much bigger than he was.

Gunvald didn't move.

"I'm just here for a drink." He sat down on a cracked bar stool.

Olin's fists were clenched so tight his knuckles were white. "Don't give me that shit, Gunvald. I know why you're here. And the screaming outside? Am I gonna find a bunch of corpses out there?"

"They were in my way."

Olin shook his head and gazed up at the ceiling. "This fucking guy," he muttered.

Gunvald shrugged.

Olin stepped so close that Gunvald could smell the beer on his breath. "You're here to bust out your buddy Darius," Olin said. "Tell me I'm wrong."

Gunvald nodded. "Since you know why I'm here, this should be quick."

Olin chuckled and loosened his fists. "You don't think I knew this day was coming the second Darius was thrown into Whitestone? That I haven't had my men preparing every single day for the moment you stepped foot in Breham?"

"I'd be more concerned if you hadn't."

Olin ran a hand through his short, tousled brown hair. "Listen, I'm only telling you this 'cause for some ungodly reason I still consider you a friend—stay away from Whitestone."

"Unless you're holding Darius somewhere else, I can't do that."

"For fuck's sake, Gunvald!" Olin kicked a stool across the tavern, sending it crashing into a nearby table. "If you want to die so bad, just stab yourself with one of your stupid swords and save everybody a lot of headache."

Gunvald waved the bartender over.

"Do not give this man a drink," Olin shouted, jabbing his thick finger at the bartender. "I swear to Fiarus if you even glance at a mug, I'll throw your ass into Whitestone faster than you can blink."

"Come on, Olin," Gunvald said. "Can't I even

get a drink?"

"You're lucky to even be sitting here right now after whatever shit I imagine you pulled outside. I could have fifty men waiting out there before you could even stand up."

"That's impressive," Gunvald said.

"You're testing my patience, Gunvald." Olin shook his head. "Have you ever sat down and really thought about how fucking stupid this whole quest of yours is?"

Gunvald had thought about it. He thought about it every day. And it never got less stupid.

"Death!" Olin continued. "The actual Death, yeah? You think you're just gonna walk up to her and what? Stab her in the face? That doesn't sound fucking insane to you?"

It did. When Gunvald was Death's Hand, he was given a fraction of her power. His strength and speed became almost inhuman. But even then, he probably never stood a chance of killing her. Now...?

"She killed my family."

"Even so, you're fucking delusional, Gunvald. You know that? Do you honestly think this is what Lea —"

Gunvald grabbed Olin's throat and pressed his

fingertips into the man's larynx. "Never say her name. You hear me?"

Olin slammed his fist down on Gunvald's forearm, knocking the hand from his neck.

"You know damn well that wasn't my fault," he said, rubbing his neck.

Gunvald clenched his fists and stood up. The few patrons who had remained out of curiosity scrambled toward the front door.

"They were your men," Gunvald growled.

"And you butchered them and got me sent to this shithole of a city. But you know what? I've made peace with that. So if you want revenge on Death for killing your family? Fine. It's your funeral. But freeing Darius? No, I don't think so. With all the shit he's pulled, especially in Central City alone, he's never getting out of Whitestone."

Gunvald turned and started for the door; his footsteps echoing loudly in the otherwise silent tavern. With his hand on the door handle, he turned around and said, "I'm not leaving here without him, Olin. Friend or not, if you get in my way, I'll kill you."

Olin's lips curled into a low growl as Gunvald swung open the tavern door and left.

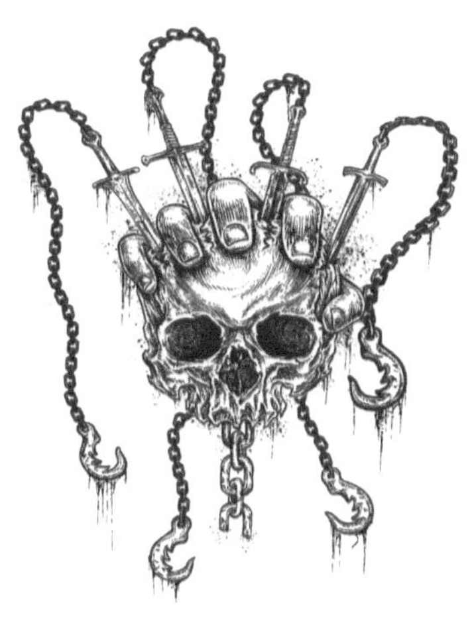

CHAPTER TWO
WHITESTONE PRISON

Whitestone Prison sat on the edge of the eastern slums. Its towering white marble walls gleamed in the moonlight behind its ten-foot iron fence. A stark contrast to the squalor surrounding it.

Central City's greatest talking point. The prison of prisons. Home to some of the most vile human beings to have ever been birthed on Anezen. Impenetrable and inescapable.

Judging by the elite force Olin had guarding the front doors, Gunvald highly fucking doubted that.

Of the two guards that were stationed at either

side of the large steel front doors, the one on the left, a formidable-looking man, was jerking his head rhythmically and rubbing his eyes, looking on the verge of losing his battle with sleep. The young kid on his right, however, had already lost that fight. He was sitting on the ground snoring. His head slumped forward and his sword and shield hanging loosely from his grasp.

If this was Olin's way of being prepared, Gunvald wasn't impressed.

An intense burning ran through Gunvald's legs as a faint red mist swirled around his calves. The chains on his swords pulled themselves close to his body as he leapt over the iron fence and set down in front of the guards. Since he'd ended his service as Hand, he felt a little dizzy using magic, and his power was fading faster than he had hoped. But that was an issue for another time.

Gunvald charged forward, clamped his hand over the formidable man's mouth, plunged a small dagger into the side of his neck, and gave it a twist. The man's spear clanked to the cobbles as he grabbed at Gunvald's arm, but it was too slippery with blood to grip.

Startled by the spear hitting the ground, the

younger guard woke up and stared at Gunvald, then at the other guard's body, which Gunvald let slump to the ground next to him. The kid grabbed his sword and tried to grab his shield, but Gunvald stomped his foot on it, almost crushing the kids hand beneath it. The kid abandoned his shield, scrambled to his feet, and pointed his blade at Gunvald.

"You... You're him..." he stammered.

"Who?"

"The... the..."

"Go home, boy."

The kid swallowed hard and held his position. "I can't let you into the prison."

Gunvald shook his head. The kid had guts, he'd give him that. But that was the only thing he had. His half-assed defensive stance and shaking arms showed a serious lack of training.

Dealing with the first guard was a given, but the last thing Gunvald wanted to do was add this kid to his ever-growing body count. He summoned Dimittis to his hand, hoping to instill enough fear into the kid to make him run.

The kid stared for a moment longer before doing just that.

Gunvald sighed. He was hoping to get in and

out of this place without much of a hassle, but that kid's gonna have the entirety of Olin's men out here within the hour. Gunvald searched the dead man's body for the prison keys and found a thick keyring in the man's left pocket. He opened the large prison doors, which swung open smoothly and without a sound, and stepped inside. A waft of stale air washed over him, and as expected, the gray, cracked walls of the hallway looked nothing like its shining marble exterior.

Not a single guard in sight. If Olin thought this was preparation, he was an idiot.

"We get in, we get out. That's it," Gunvald muttered, not sure if to himself, or the wretched scraps of steel dragging behind him.

The swords clattered loudly as Gunvald walked down the dimly lit hallway, but still no guards. The thought that he was walking into a trap had briefly entered his mind, but he quickly shoved it away. Olin was running a shit operation, as usual. He was almost certain that whatever guards were here had no clue Gunvald was even a thing they needed to worry about.

A cacophony of laughter and screaming spilled up from a descending staircase at the end of the hallway. He didn't bother to gather up his swords as he walked down, the noise below was more than loud enough to drown out the sound of the damned things banging down the staircase.

Gunvald stopped at a wide stone platform a few steps above a corridor between two rows of cells, of which two of the doors hung open. Three guards were slouched in wooden chairs on the left side of the platform. A fourth guard, with a similar build to Gunvald's, stood in the doorway to a small room just behind the three men. Their bloodshot eyes and the scattered liqueur bottles on the small table in front of them confirmed Olin was full of shit. Nobody had planned for Gunvald. Hell, until Gunvald stepped into the Wretched Dove earlier, Olin likely thought he was dead.

The laughter stopped. "Who the hell are you?" one of the guards bellowed.

Another guard, a thin man with an eyepatch that barely covered the scarred lump of flesh beneath it, rose from his chair and steadied himself on the table. "You're him, ain't cha? The death guy?"

At least one of them knew who he was.

The other two guards staggered up. One had a jagged scar down his cheek and looked on the verge of vomiting. The other, a flabby mess of a man, looked so drunk that Gunvald doubted the man even knew he was in a prison, let alone supposed to be guarding it.

All three men fumbled to draw their swords. Dimittis and Obitus coiled into Gunvald's hands. Eyepatch was closest. Gunvald drove Dimittis into his gut and stabbed Obitus's broken, jagged blade into his neck.

He sidestepped Scarface's lumbering, wild swing, and the man stumbled and knocked over their table, sending the liqueur bottles crashing to the floor.

Scarface tried to steady himself, but Gunvald plunged Dimittis deep into the guard's chest, painting the air with a mist of blood.

The guard in the doorway didn't give a shit about the other guards; that much was clear. He stood there smirking and staring at Gunvald.

The flabby guard tried to raise his sword, but got it caught under a leg of the flipped table, and he stumbled forward. Gunvald dropped Obitus, grabbed Dimittis with both hands, and cut deep into the flabby man's stomach, spilling his guts onto the stone floor.

The flabby man staggered around the platform, tripped over his own guts, and tumbled down the stairs to the corridor between the cells.

"Not bad," the guy in the doorway said. "But I've seen better."

Gunvald shrugged. Then he kicked the last standing chair at the guy and called Cinis to his hands. The man jumped out of the way of the chair and drew his sword. Gunvald swung Cinis at his head. The man parried, and their steel blades clanged together.

Gunvald spun away and kicked him in the gut, sending him sprawling into the wall. Then Gunvald charged in, kneed the man in the face, and felt the satisfying crunch of his nose breaking. The jackass pushed Gunvald's knee aside, rolled to his feet, and wiped the blood from his face with his sleeve. The guard lunged forward, swinging wildly. Obitus swung itself up from the ground and deflected the blow while Gunvald stuck Cinis through the man's gut and yanked the blade up and out with a sickening squelch.

Gunvald dropped Cinis and stared at Obitus, lying on the stone floor, glazed with blood.

What the fuck was that? In the ten years he'd been burdened with the swords, they'd whispered incessantly in his head for blood, but not once had they ever done anything on their own.

They'd stayed out of his way when he moved, sure, but he'd always assumed it was by some subconscious order he didn't realize he was giving. But moving on their own to block an attack? If this had anything to do with his waning powers as a Hand, then he was quickly running out of time.

A cell door slammed. A tall, lanky, twenty-somethingish man glanced up at him from the cell corridor.

"Oh, shit," the guard said. He clumsily unsheathed his sword. "Addy?"

Great. More fucking distractions.

Gunvald approached the stairs leading down to the cells. Thanks to Obitus, he had forgotten about the two open cells and the guards that were likely in them.

One of them, apparently Addy, who appeared around the same age as the lanky man, stepped out from the closest open cell.

"Look," Gunvald growled, walking down the steps, "I'm only gonna say this once. You leave, or you die."

Judging by their faces, Gunvald already knew how this was going to go. The lanky man would disappear like smoke, but Addy? Yeah, he was going to die tonight.

"I don't think so, old man," Addy said.

The swords whispered in Gunvald's mind—*just kill them and get it over with.*

Hell, the swords might just do it themselves at

this point, who the fuck knows?

As expected, the lanky man dropped his sword and raised his hands above his head. "I... I'm going... please... don't... don't kill me."

Gunvald heard a sharp inhale of breath as he walked past the man without a second glance. The man fled up the stairs, footsteps pattering into the distance.

"Pussy," Addy said.

Something about the arrogance in Addy's stance pissed Gunvald off. The way Addy shifted his weight. The way he twirled his sword. Not to mention his stupid fucking grin.

Addy glanced down, apparently to watch Dimittis's chains crawl around Gunvald's arm and pull its hilt into his left hand. What he should have been watching was the dagger Gunvald slipped into his right hand.

Gunvald flung the dagger spinning through the air into Addy's Adam's apple. Addy dropped his sword and grasped futilely at the hilt in his neck. Blood poured down his chest, and he let out one last gasp before he crumpled to the floor. A loud outburst of cheering and hooting erupted from the cells.

Gunvald stepped over Addy and walked down the corridor, looking for Darius. Some prisoners cheered him; others begged to be freed; still others just stared from the backs of their cells.

In the second to last cell on the right, Gunvald found Darius Ryker, the Broken Gunmage.

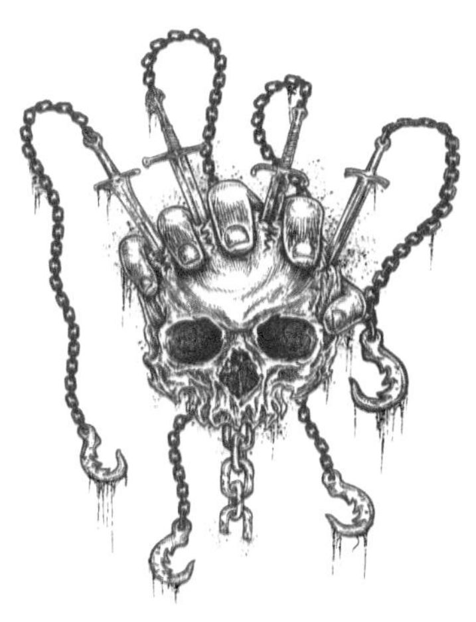

CHAPTER THREE
WHITESTONE PRISON

Gunvald struggled in the dim lighting to make out Darius, who sat hunched in the far corner of his cell, his head bowed. Darius's usually well-groomed black hair was now a disheveled set of locs, his dark skin was ashy, and he had purple welts on his face and arms. Gunvald tried a few keys from the ring and found the one that opened the cell door. Darius did not move.

"After all the shit I just went through," Gunvald said, stepping into the cell, "if you're gonna make me carry your ass outta here, I'm just gonna leave."

"Gunvald?" Darius asked.

Darius dragged himself to his feet with the help

of the cell wall. His wrists were clamped in heavy steel manacles. He took a few weak steps forward and head-butted Gunvald squarely between the eyes, narrowly missing his nose.

"What the fuck?" Gunvald took a step back.

"That's for leaving me in here for so long."

Gunvald rubbed his head. "For the record, I didn't even know you were in here until a week ago. And I didn't get you thrown in here. You did that on your own."

"The fuck I did. What I did should have got me thrown into Garrison, or maybe Newgate. Being friends with your dumbass got me thrown into this fucking hellhole."

Gunvald shrugged. "Listen, for what it's worth, I'm sorry."

He was only half sincere, but it was the best he could do.

Darius shook his head and smiled. "See? That wasn't so hard, was it? Does it erase four months of fucking torture? No, but it's nice to hear." Darius held his chained wrists out in front of him. "Now get me out of these fucking things."

Gunvald held up the ring full of keys.

Darius sighed. "We're gonna be here all fucking

night."

Heavy footsteps echoed down the corridor. Darius's eyes went wide. "Please tell me you already took out Horace?"

"I guess not," Gunvald muttered. "Here."

He handed Darius the keyring and exited the cell.

"Wait..." Darius said

Gunvald ignored him, stepped out of the cell, and was immediately knocked to the ground. He rolled and came to a stop on one knee. He reached his right arm back for Obitus.

A massive, muscular hulk towered over him. A thick blanket of long gray hair nearly obscured his pale face, smashed-in nose, and giant underbite, but did nothing to cover up his rancid stench.

Gunvald shook his head to clear it. The half-ogre smiled, a large glob of drool dripping down onto his chin.

"Horace, I presume," Gunvald said.

Horace pulled an enormous studded club from his belt and hoisted onto his shoulder. Gunvald had only fought a half-ogre once before and barely survived. Even with his Hand powers, he almost got his head squeezed to a fucking pulp. Now? He'd be lucky if he made it out of this with all his limbs still attached.

"Hey Horace," Darius yelled. Then he jumped forward and smashed his head into Horace's face.

Horace grunted, lifted Darius into the air by his neck, and slammed him down next to Gunvald.

"Really?" Gunvald said. "Another headbutt?"

Darius raised an eyebrow and held up his hands to show Gunvald his chained wrists.

"Just stay out of the way."

Gunvald clambered up and lunged at the half-ogre. Horace raised his club and swung it down. Gunvald met it with Obitus in a shower of sparks. Horace roared, swatted Obitus away with a giant, gnarled hand, and swung his club again. Gunvald stumbled sideways and narrowly avoided it. Horace's follow-through tipped him off balance, and Gunvald stabbed him in the side.

Blood splattered across the open door of Darius's cell and across the stone floor. Horace bounced off a cell's bars, regained his footing, and displayed his fucked-up teeth in a wide grin.

Gunvald tossed Obitus on the floor, summoned Cinis, and swung it with both hands. The blade clashed against Horace's club so hard Gunvald's arms went numb. Horace tried to grab him, but Gunvald twisted away and swung Cinis at Horace's chest.

Horace caught the blade with his bare hand and laughed. Gunvald tried to pull it away. His eyes stung from the stench leaking from every pore of the half-ogre's body.

Darius lunged at Horace from behind and slammed his manacled fists into the half-ogre's lower back. Horace staggered forward and turned around to attack the gunmage.

Kill him! Bleed him!

Gunvald found himself seething, clenching his teeth. He jumped onto Horace's back, wrapped Cinis's chain around the half-ogre's giant neck, and wrenched back. Horace flung himself backwards, slamming Gunvald into a cell door.

"Squeeze, damn it," Gunvald told the sword. "You give no shits about doing it to me."

Horace slammed him again. Gunvald grunted, and his grip on Cinis's chain loosened. "C'mon, you bastard piece of tin." He pulled with all his might. At last, Cinis started squeezing.

With one hand on the chain, Gunvald summoned Obitus into the other and slammed the broken blade into Horace's side and twisted. Green blood sprayed into the air. Horace roared and flailed around, throwing Gunvald from his back and sending him crashing into Darius. Then Horace stopped roaring, stopped doing anything, and toppled forward, face-first on the stone floor.

The inmates whooped and whistled and howled.

Gunvald rolled off Darius.

"Hey, you good man?" Darius asked. Hands still chained, he dropped the keyring on the floor. "You look a little tired."

Gunvald lay back on the stone floor. "Shut up."

Darius slammed his foot into Horace's head. "That's what you get, asshole." Then he started rifling through the pockets of the half-ogre's grimy, blood-drenched tunic with his chained hands.

"What the hell are you doing?" Gunvald asked.

Darius pulled a small keyring from Horace's pocket and dangled it in front of Gunvald's face. "I sure as shit ain't waiting for you to try every fucking key on that monstrosity of a keyring you brought in here."

Gunvald snatched the keys from Darius and unlocked the manacles.

Darius rubbed his wrists. "Damn, that feels good."

"Here." Gunvald tossed Darius the small keyring. "Make yourself useful." He gestured towards the other cells.

Darius hesitated. "Uh... you know most of these people can't be trusted, right?"

"We're gonna need them."

"Alright. I just think— wait, what do you mean we're gonna need them? Need them for what?"

"To get out of here."

Darius sighed. "Let me guess, you ran into Olin?"

Gunvald shrugged.

"And he's waiting outside for us right now, isn't he?"

"Probably," Gunvald replied.

Darius shook his head. "Alright, it's your call, but if you want my suggestion, you leave ol' Cassidy in cell two right where he is. That guy's worse than you when it comes to killin people."

"We need them all," Gunvald said.

Darius shrugged. "Whatever you say. It's your funeral, and everyone else's..."

* * *

It took about ten minutes for Darius to unlock all of the cells and release forty-six of the most wretched souls ever born and even less time for Gunvald to convince them to go along with his escape plan and lead them back to the steel front doors of the prison.

The chance at freedom, not to mention Gunvald's display of slaughtering the guards and strangling Horace, made for a convincing argument against refusing.

"Wait for my signal. Got it?" he told them.

A few of the men grunted; others said nothing. The one named Cassidy licked his lips and smiled.

Darius whispered, "I hope you know what you're doing."

Gunvald pushed open the doors. The morning sun blasted his eyes, and he put up his hand to shield them. When they adjusted, he saw Olin Tibout standing by the fence with about thirty armed watchmen.

CHAPTER FOUR
BREHAM CITY SLUMS

"Do us all a favor, Gunvald," Olin called out, "just go back inside."

"You know I can't do that, Olin."

The watchmen shifted their weight and tightened their grips on their weapons.

Olin paced back and forth. "You're really making things difficult, Gunvald, you know that? Last offer. Darius goes back into Whitestone, and you get to walk out of here."

The watchmen muttered among themselves; one shook his head.

"Not gonna happen," Gunvald said.

Olin threw his arms up. "You know what? Don't say I didn't try, alright?"

Gunvald kicked back against the prison doors. A second later, the prison doors were flung open and slammed against the prisons walls with a loud clang. The prisoners hollered and howled as they rushed out of the prison, armed with chains, iron bars, and weapons they'd taken from the dead guards. The watchmen raised their weapons and stepped back while the inmates rushed towards them.

Gunvald and Darius walked towards the prison gate. One inmate, a lazy-eyed fuck, either too stupid to remember the plan or just taking his shot, raised a steel pipe above his head and charged Gunvald.

Darius ducked out of the way. Obitus came into Gunvald's hand. He held it up and blocked the pipe with a loud clang. Then he cracked the inmate in the face with a left hook.

The cock-eyed bastard lurched sideways, and Gunvald kicked him in the left knee. The inmate dropped to the walkway. Gunvald grabbed the man's head and drove his knee into his face, then let him fall to the ground.

"Shoulda stuck to the plan, asshole," Darius

said.

Gunvald and Darius continued walking towards the prison gate.

"Do you know what you've fucking done?!" Olin yelled.

Gunvald nodded. "Subdued a violent escaped prisoner for you?"

Cock-eye was still rolling on the ground holding his face.

A group of five watchmen came running up the street behind Olin with their weapons drawn. "Sir!" one yelled.

Olin clenched his hands, glared at Gunvald, then addressed the guard. "Let them go."

"But, sir–"

"I said, let them go!" Olin yelled. He pointed a thick finger toward the courtyard where the other guards were struggling against the inmates. "Just get in there and help!" He turned back to Gunvald. "You'd better hope I don't see you again."

"You won't," Gunvald said. He dropped Obitus to the ground.

Olin hollered, "when it's all said and done, you're gonna wish you stayed in Whitestone."

Darius laughed. "In your dreams, Olin."

"A lot of people want to get their hands on you, Darius," Olin said. "Don't say I didn't warn you."

Gunvald and Darius walked through the gate.

* * *

It hurt Gunvald's side to walk, though nothing seemed broken. The stench of Breham still lingered in the air, but at least the daylight made it easier to navigate the shit-littered streets. It was also silent. A rare occurrence when Darius was around.

"Be straight with me, Gun," Darius said. "I'm not stupid. I know why you broke me out. Just tell me you have a plan, any kind of plan."

"Just a target," Gunvald said.

Darius sighed. "And your powers?"

Gunvald didn't reply. He didn't have to. Darius knew the answer, he just wanted some kind of assurance they weren't marching to their death unprepared, which was exactly what they were doing.

They continued to walk in silence, dust blowing in their faces as they exited the slums and onto the barren, dusty plains that surrounded Breham. A few minutes later they reached a small cluster of dead trees where Gunvald had tied two horses before entering

Breham, both Arabians, one black, the other chestnut.

"At least tell me you got me a piece or two." Darius said.

Gunvald walked up to the black Arabian with a striking white blaze on its face, and ran his hand along the horse's neck.

Darius patted the other side of the horse's neck. "You still hanging around with this guy, Nomad?"

"Here." Gunvald pulled a leather-wrapped bundle out of Nomad's saddlebag and tossed it at Darius.

Darius unwrapped the bundle, and his eyes widened. He hung the holster belt over his forearm and weighed the pair of sleek, dark silver spell pistols in his hands. The barrels of the pistols were distinctively thick, angular shaped. The striking plate was a gold spell ring rather than the more common cylinder spell core. Darius looked at Gunvald. "Are these what I think they are?"

Gunvald shook his head and stroked Nomad's neck. "And here we go. I told you this would happen."

"Mage cannons? Seriously?" Darius spun the guns around his fingers. "Don't be playing with me right now, man. Are they real? Man, if you're fucking with me, you better tell me now."

"They're real."

"Seriously? Like mythical, tap into the spirit realm, overpowered as shit, serious?"

Gunvald swung onto Nomad's saddle and sighed. "Yes. Now, can you get on your damn horse so we can get out of here?"

"What tier? One? Two?"

"Four."

"Tier-four mage cannons? Now I know you're fucking with me. Tier four? That's practically a god-level artifact." Darius twirled the pistols again, then stopped. "Wait, they're not gonna sprout chains and try to suck out my soul, are they?"

"No, but I'm hoping they'll be enough for you to put a hole through Amaya's fucking chest. Now, for fuck's sake, get on your horse or I'm giving you back to Olin."

"Okay, okay, geez." Darius strapped on the holster belt, secured the mage cannons, and mounted the chestnut Arabian. "Don't get your braies in a bunch."

Gunvald turned Nomad toward the dirt road that led away from Breham. Darius steered his horse to follow, left hand lingering on the handle of the mage cannon on his hip.

"I bet I could take out half of Central City with one shot," Darius said.

"That's the kinda shit that gets you thrown back into Whitestone."

Darius shrugged. "If it's still standing."

Gunvald glared at Darius.

"I'm just sayin." Darius took his hand off the gun. "So who are we going after?"

Gunvald shook his head. "Trust me, you don't want to know."

"Don't give me that broody, doom and gloom shit. Just tell me who it is."

Gunvald paused. "King Adder."

It wasn't a complete lie. They would most likely have to fight King Adder. He just wasn't anyone Death would get off her lazy ass to come collect. Darius couldn't know the actual target was Adder's daughter Ceres, not yet.

"The Black General? Really?" Darius said.

"I told you, you didn't want to know."

Darius shook his head. "Fuck me, man. You couldn't find anybody other than the damn Black General? You might as well put killing Velena on your list while we're at it, since you're thinking up impossible shit to do," Darius said.

The goddess of Helios. And Amaya's boss. Maybe. If this plan went to shit.

"He's got someone who can bring the dead back to life," Gunvald said.

"Necromancy?"

"Not quite," Gunvald said. "More like putting a spirit back into its body."

"Get the fuck outta here. Are you serious?"

Gunvald nodded.

"Well, shit," Darius said. "But why Adder? Why not go after the necromancer, or whatever they are?"

"I couldn't get any solid leads, so we'll have to get to them through Adder."

Another lie. Gunvald had no doubt it was Ceres, and he knew Amaya would come out for her. She had a soft spot for manipulating children. But until the girl turned thirteen, her magic was weak, and Gunvald was certain Amaya didn't know about her yet.

"Well, shit," Darius said. "Anything else you wanna add to make it even more difficult?"

"If you want out, just say so."

"Oh, don't give me that bullshit. You know I don't have a choice." Darius hung his head. "Leanna was like family. Your boy too. You don't get to do what Amaya did and walk away. That shit shouldn't have happened. We held up our end of the fucking deal."

Gunvald stared straight ahead as they rode, not listening to anything after Darius mentioned Leanna. Memories of his family filled his mind. The look in Leanna's eyes in that last moment of life. The screaming of his boy as Amaya took his life. Those were things better left forgotten.

"If we're gonna do this," Darius looked down, "can we at least stop somewhere and get some clothes? My dick's just swinging in the wind here."

Gunvald eyed Darius's dirtied gray prison rags and the exquisite leather holster around his waist.

"You do look kind of ridiculous."

"That's what I'm sayin."

"We can find some clothes in Endwyn."

"Endwyn?" Darius raised an eyebrow. "Why Endwyn?"

"One, it's only half a day's ride from here, and two, there's something there I need to pick up."

"Like what? More godly artifacts? Or better yet, a giant fucking army?"

"More like a giant fucking bear."

"Oh, come on!" Darius tossed his arms up. "Why, man? Just why?"

"We need him."

"No, we don't," Darius said. "He's always fucking with me."

Gunvald shrugged. Bear was a beast of a man who could easily crush a man's skull with one hand. He also had a thing for Darius. But if they were gonna have any hope of pulling this thing off, they'd need his help.

"Fuck me," Darius muttered. "I wonder if Olin's offer still stands."

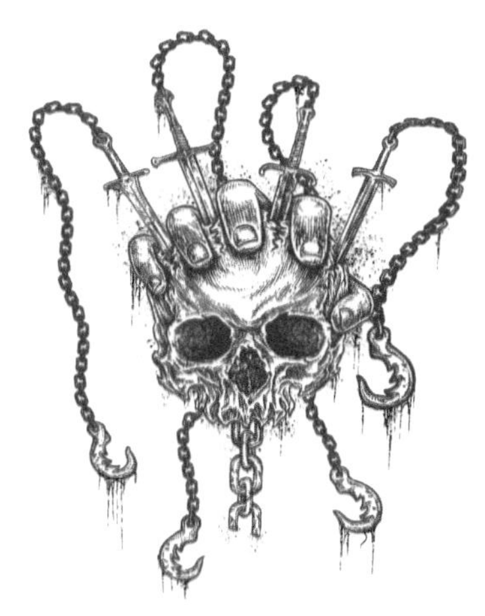

CHAPTER FIVE
VILLAGE OF ALRYNE
TWENTY YEARS EARLIER

"Gunvald!" his mother yelled through the kitchen window.

The sky was overcast, and the smell of petrichor was heavy in the air. Gunvald tuned her out and continued his half-cut drills against the wooden pell in his backyard.

He was determined to complete his practice before the inevitable downpour. His dad always told him that heroes were not born, but created through perseverance and determination. If Gunvald wanted to be like the heroes in his father's stories, he had to put in the effort.

His mother yelled again. "Gunvald!"

Gunvald sighed. He gave the pell one last half-strike. "What?"

"Go get your father. Dinner's almost ready."

"Fine." Gunvald huffed. He dropped his wooden sword and wiped the sweat off his brow with his sleeve.

Gunvald didn't particularly feel like making the ten-minute walk to the other side of the village, where his father was working the fields near the old mine. Mostly because he dreaded passing the Watkyn house.

Gunvald looked more like a fourteen or fifteen-year-old than a ten-year-old, and Rowan Watkyn and his band of assholes always teased him about it. The teasing didn't bother him as much as the exasperating way Rowan and his friends danced around him while they did it.

As he neared the Watkyn's house, he expected to see Rowan's equally asinine father lazily tossing hay while his mother sang loud and off-key from inside the house, but there was none of that.

Seeing their house apparently abandoned was unusual, considering they didn't have the money to go anywhere else. Not that anyone else in Alryne was faring much better, thanks to the ongoing war.

A light drizzle started as Gunvald passed the old mine, and he thought he heard thunder rolling in. When he got to the fence around the field, he climbed up and waved his arm. "Dad!"

His father wiped the sweat from his head, set down his hoe, waved and walked over to Gunvald. "Dinner ready?"

"Yeah, Mom sent me to get you."

"Alright, tell her I'm—" The thunder sound rumbled again. His father's brow furrowed, and his eyes widened.

Somebody on the field yelled, "Raiders!"

Gunvald spun around. A large dust cloud billowed in the distance.

"Go home," his father said. "Get your mother and hide in the crawl space. I'll be there as soon as I can."

"What? No! I can fight."

"No! Go home, get your mother, and hide. Do you hear me?"

Gunvald nodded. "Yeah."

"Alright. Go! And be careful."

The low rumbling turned into hoofbeats and

hollering. Gunvald hopped off the fence and sprinted toward his house, shouting a warning at every house he passed.

A villager screamed as Gunvald reached the halfway point past the Smitton house. Then another. Gunvald's heart pounded. He ran faster than he ever thought he could. He had to get his mother into the crawl space, then he could get his father's sword and fight.

He heard the hooves clomping behind him as his house came into sight and glanced over his shoulder. A man with a thick red beard was riding hard towards him, short sword in hand.

Gunvald dove into a pile of hay to the right of the road. The raider cursed as he rode past.

Gunvald's heart raced. He searched for anything he could use as a weapon, found two weathered wooden pitchforks leaning on the fence behind the hay pile, grabbed one, and scrambled to his feet.

The raider swung his horse around and charged. Gunvald stepped into the road, holding his pitchfork up. The raider took a swing; Gunvald ducked and tried to stab him with the pitchfork, but was too slow.

The raider brought the horse around again. Frustrated, Gunvald hurled the pitchfork at the horse's face. The horse reared up and tossed the raider from the saddle. Gunvald picked up the second pitchfork, ran at the man, and stabbed him in the gut.

Two pitchfork tines broke off in the raider's belly. He writhed in agony, rolling on the road and groaning. Gunvald expected to be afraid or revolted seeing the man bleed out, but to his surprise, he didn't really care.

"Gunvald!" His mother's yell snapped him out of his trance. He dropped the pitchfork and ran toward his house. His mother was waving frantically in the front doorway.

"Are you okay?!" she screamed. "You're not hurt, are you?"

"I'm fine," he told her. "We have to hide in the crawl space."

"Where's your father?"

"I don't know. He just told me to run."

His mother pushed him into the house. She took one last glance outside, slammed the door shut, and slid the locking bolt into place. "Quick, get to the crawlspace," she said. Then she disappeared into the bedroom.

Gunvald flung away the frayed brown rug from the living room floor and pulled up the hatch.

Something slammed against the front door. The door cracked and splintered and the blade of an axe stuck through it.

"Mom!" Gunvald yelled.

His mother rushed out of the bedroom with one of his father's short swords in her hand. She pushed Gunvald towards the musty crawlspace. "Go! Don't come out, no matter what."

Gunvald had one foot in the crawlspace when a large chunk of wood fell from the front door. Then another. Then a leather boot shattered what remained. A large raider stomped into the house. Gunvald's mother took a clumsy swing at him, which he easily dodged. Then he grabbed a fistful of her hair and threw her onto the floor.

"Mom!"

Gunvald climbed out of the crawlspace and lunged at the raider. He punched the raider in the side, then again, before the raider grabbed Gunvald by the throat and lifted him into the air. Gunvald kicked at the man's body and slammed his fists on the man's arm, but the raider's grip held firm.

His mother scrambled up and smashed a wooden chair on the raider's head. The man lost his balance, fell forward, and sent Gunvald sprawling onto the floor, his head slamming into the hatch of the crawlspace.

* * *

Gunvald woke up on the cold ground under his house, covered in dirt, his head pounding. Slivers of light seeped through the cracks in the wooden walls. He held his breath and listened. There was only silence. He got up on his knees and tried to push the hatch open, but it wouldn't budge. He took a chance and called out, "Mom?"

Nothing. Gunvald shuffled around, sat on his ass, and kicked a wooden wall plank. The plank creaked then thudded to the ground outside. He squeezed through the narrow opening and climbed to his feet.

The air smelled of smoke. He sprinted to the backyard and grabbed his wooden practice sword off the ground. It wouldn't stop a raider's axe, but it was better than nothing.

He crept around to the front doorway. "Mom?" No answer. He stepped over the splintered planks and into the house.

Tables and chairs were broken and scattered around the room. Most of their cabinets had been emptied, while others were knocked over and shattered. His mother's lifeless body lay over the crawlspace hatch, her face more purple than white, a stab wound in her side, her dress half torn off.

Gunvald heard footsteps behind him.

He climbed over the debris and rushed into the bedroom, tightening his grip on his practice sword.

The footsteps were now in the living room.

He wouldn't let the raiders get away with this. He stepped into the doorway and held up his wooden sword.

A woman was standing at the far side of the room, gazing at his mother's body, her hand over her mouth. She wore a tight black silk bliaut and had long black hair, wide cheekbones, and a narrow chin. She was more beautiful than anyone Gunvald had ever seen.

"Get away from her!" he yelled.

The woman didn't even flinch. She leaned down and grasped his mother's wrist.

"I said get away from her!"

Again, she ignored him.

She helped his mother to her feet, even though her body still lay motionless on the floor.

"Mo... Mom?"

The woman looked at Gunvald. "You are quite

the anomaly, Gunvald Reistad."

"How did you—"

The woman held her finger to her lips. "Shhh. We'll talk in a moment."

His mother didn't look at him. Her lips moved, but no sound came out. The black-haired woman, however, seemed to hear every word. She nodded. "I will."

The woman touched his mother's head, whispered, and right before Gunvald's eyes, his mother vanished in a burst of radiant light.

"No!" Gunvald yelled.

"Be at ease, Gunvald Reistad. She is heading to a better place," the woman said in a soothing tone that brought a strange sort of comfort to Gunvald. "Now, walk with me."

"No! Bring her back!"

"Unfortunately, that is beyond my power."

She moved elegantly across the room; her flowing dress skimming over the scattered debris.

Gunvald wiped the tears from his eyes, looked at his mother's body one last time, and followed the woman out the front door.

The usually bustling village was eerily quiet. He trailed a few feet behind the woman, looking for something more threatening than a beat-up wooden sword.

"Who are you?"

"I have been called by many names, although lately I've come to prefer the name Amaya." The woman walked to the front door of the Longgust's house, pushed the door open, and stepped inside. Gunvald approached the doorway and cautiously peered in.

The woman delicately lifted what Gunvald assumed was Mrs. Longgust's spirit from her body. Again, they conversed in silence, and then Mrs. Longgust's spirit vanished in a brilliant ball of white light. Gunvald felt a surge of courage and decided it was time to speak up.

"You're Death, aren't you?"

"I prefer Amaya." The woman smiled.

"You don't look like the stories."

She stared into Gunvald's eyes. "I have found this guise brings a sense of comfort to those on their way to Astrum. The ones bound for Helos, however..."

Amaya smiled and approached him. Gunvald tightened his grip on his sword. But she walked right past him, laughing gently.

"Be at ease. I did not come here for the living." With a wave, she beckoned him to follow her. "But I wouldn't mind taking you with me."

With a firm grip on his wooden sword, he followed her out the door to the road. He knew he couldn't fight Death, but the sword felt good in his hand.

"What do you mean, take me with you?" he finally asked.

"The veil between this realm and the spirit realm is one that mortals should not be able to pierce. You should not be able to see me, Gunvald Reistad, nor the spirits of the dead, and yet here we are, having a pleasant conversation. I could use someone like you."

"That doesn't answer my question."

Amaya didn't reply.

The body of the raider Gunvald had stabbed with the pitchfork lay in the road. Amaya stopped next to it. In an instant, the elegance was gone, and in it's place was a creature of living nightmare. The skin on her face, once full and vibrant, was thin and taut.

Her deep brown eyes were hollow voids. She wore a tattered black robe instead of her silk bliaut, which billowed around her, as if caught in a breeze, though there was none. Spiked chains twisted and writhed from her sleeves and torso.

She plunged her hand into the raider's chest.

Gunvald could hear her ripping and tearing inside his body. When she pulled her hand from the raider's chest, the man's spirit came out with it.

In her other hand, a long black scythe materialized from a cloud of thick black smoke. The spirit's eyes went wide, and his mouth opened in a silent scream. He tried to pull away but couldn't.

Death hacked off the spirit's arms, then its legs. While the raider's cries were silent, Gunvald's mind filled in the sound. He turned his head and covered his ears. A few seconds later, Amaya softly touched his shoulder. Startled, Gunvald spun on his heels, and fell to the ground, his sword falling from his hand. Amaya stood above him, as beautiful as before. She reached out her hand to him. He hesitated, but took it.

Gunvald couldn't help but glance at the raider's body. It was completely stripped of flesh and surrounded by a pool of blood. The raider's bony face was still frozen in a scream. He picked up his wooden sword.

"Is everyone in the village dead?" Gunvald asked.

"Not everyone."

"My father?"

"Yes, I'm sorry."

He had expected as much. Gunvald stabbed his wooden sword into the dirt and cursed. After a few second he asked Amaya, "What did my mother say before you sent her to Astrum?"

"The last words of the dead are not meant for mortal ears," Amaya replied.

"She was my mother. I deserve to know."

Amaya smiled. "She asked me to keep you safe. Although with your gifts, I would like to do more. Consider, would you rather stay here, one of the few survivors of a village soon to be forgotten, or would you come with me, and I'll give you the power to exact the revenge you desire, and more."

Revenge had never crossed Gunvald's mind until now, but he was intrigued by the thought. He walked back to the remains of the raider, laid his wooden sword on the dirt road, and picked up the man's crude short sword. The hilt felt smooth and cold in his hand. It also felt right.

DARIUS

CHAPTER SIX
TOWN OF ENDWYN

Endwyn was a slightly nicer place than Breham, but that was a low bar. The houses and buildings had crudely patched walls and dingy, scum-covered windows, but at least the streets were clean, and the air didn't smell like a rotting corpse in an outhouse.

Endwyn was another casualty of the Sunset War, which, despite ending five years before, had left wounds that refused to heal and people who refused to care.

Gunvald and Darius reached Endwyn about midday. As they walked down the center of the town's only road, the townspeople stared at them from the windows of their squat homes, stables, and shops. The ones on the street just glared and gave them a wide berth.

Their attention initially fell on Darius, but it quickly shifted to Gunvald, and then to the swords carelessly scraping against the ground behind him.

Darius frowned and pulled his ragged shirt over the torn crotch of his pants. "Can we get some clothes already?"

"Relax," Gunvald told him. "They've got more important things to worry about than your dick hanging out."

"Says the fully clothed man."

Gunvald pointed to a small building on the left. A weathered wooden sign showing a worn pair of scissors hung precariously by a single chain over the wooden door.

"That's what I'm talkin about," Darius said. "I hope you've got some coin on you."

Gunvald sighed.

* * *

"Get the fuck outta here," Darius yanked off the hood of his new cloak. "I know he has a hard-on for cookies and shit, but a bakery? Really?"

"Apparently."

The sun was high overhead when Gunvald and Darius reached the bakery. The two-story gray stone structure looked well built and well maintained. A large wooden sign hung over the doorway: Bear's Bakery. The smell of fresh bread wafted from the windows.

The chains connected to Gunvald's swords unwrapped themselves from his body and retracted into the sword's pommels without a fight. Or a command, for that matter. Gunvald stared back at the swords lying in the street. He couldn't help but feel they were fucking with him.

"You just gonna leave them there?" Darius asked.

Gunvald shrugged.

"Fine by me. Those things freak me out anyway." Darius shuddered. "Returning to more important issues, this town is an ass hair away from oblivion, and this fucking guy opens up a fancy-ass bakery?"

Gunvald shrugged again and opened the heavy bakery door. The intense smell of yeast enveloped him, mixed with a hint of cinnamon.

An array of trencher breads lay on a small

counter to the left of the door. Cookies and tarts sat on a small table beside it. A case on the far wall next to a back doorway contained even more bread.

Darius gaped at the goods. "This is like Central City levels of baking."

"They're my most loyal customers," Bear said as he emerged from the back doorway. He was a good foot taller than Gunvald and twice as wide, a towering figure made entirely of muscle. A thick beard and mustache, a new addition since the last time Gunvald had seen him, covered the lower half of his face.

"And what can I get you fine gentlemen today?" He approached, looking Darius up and down. "You're looking good, D, a bit thinner than usual, but maybe I can fatten you up."

"Man, don't even start," Darius groaned.

"I heard you got snagged in Central City," Bear said, stopping in front of the counter. "What the hell were you doing up there?"

"I'm not even gonna go into it with you. Besides, it wasn't my fault."

"Sure it wasn't." Bear looked at Gunvald. "You wouldn't be here to buy some sweets, would you?"

"The bread does smell good," Gunvald said.

Bear sighed. "At least give me a hug." He held

his thick arms out.

Gunvald obliged the big man's request without hesitation. "It's good to see you, Bear."

"You too, Gunvald. I just wish it were under better circumstances."

Bear let Gunvald go and extended his arms towards Darius. "Bring it in, sweetness."

Darius shook his head and waved his hands in front of him. "Nah, I'm good, man."

Bear shrugged. "I figured it was only a matter of time until the two of you showed up, all things considered." He walked over to a shelf, the wooden floor creaking below him, grabbed a small, round loaf of bread and tossed it to Darius. "On the house, pretty boy."

Darius caught the bread and took a big bite. Crumbs fell from his lips into his beard. Then, mouth full of food, he mumbled, "You hear about this necromancy shit, too?" He stopped chewing for a second. "Bear, this is really fucking good, man."

"Thank you," Bear said. "And yeah, I got the message." Bear glanced at Gunvald.

"Well, that makes things a little easier," Darius shoved another piece of bread in his mouth. "Speaking of easier," Darius drew one of the mage cannons from its holster and deftly spun it in his free hand. "Check these bad boys out, Bear. Tier-four mage cannons, baby."

Bear barely glanced at the guns. "And let me guess, you haven't stopped talking about them since you got them?"

Darius abruptly ceased his twirling.

Gunvald sighed. "Yep."

"Screw you guys," Darius said, and holstered the cannons. "You fuckers can sit here and figure out the little stuff like necromancers and shit. I'm gonna head out and do the big boy work, like finding us a way through the wastelands, 'cause we sure as shit ain't getting through Adder's checkpoints on our own."

Darius snatched three fruit tarts from the table by the front door. "For the road," he said, and walked out the door.

"Still the same Darius," Bear said.

"Yep."

"You're not gonna tell him the truth about Adder's necromancer?" Bear asked.

"Nope. And you're not either."

Bear shook his head. "That's fucked up. He should know what he's getting into."

"If anything can kill Amaya, it's those cannons.

If he knows Adder's kid's the one we're after, he'll try to stop us."

"Of course he would. And he should. She's just a kid, after all."

"Yeah, well, exceptions have to be made."

Bear pursed his lips and turned away. "You've changed, my friend, and not for the better. The old Gunvald would never kill a kid... on purpose. When I got your letter, I actually prayed to every god imaginable that it wasn't true. But I guess the gods don't care about us little people."

Gunvald didn't reply. He knew Bear was right. He shook his head. "Damn it."

Bear walked back through the rear doorway, and Gunvald could hear him rustling through something. "Where the fuck is it," he heard Bear mutter. "Ahh..."

Bear came back into the room holding a wooden crate filled with beer bottles.

"I was saving these for a special occasion, but I guess today will have to do," Bear said. He grabbed a bottle and handed it to Gunvald. "We should really tell him, Gun. It'll save us a lot of trouble later on."

Gunvald grunted. He didn't like keeping secrets from Darius, but it wasn't hard. Darius never stopped talking about himself. Truth be told, he didn't like the idea of killing a kid either. Still, Amaya had to die. If that meant killing Adder's daughter, then so be it.

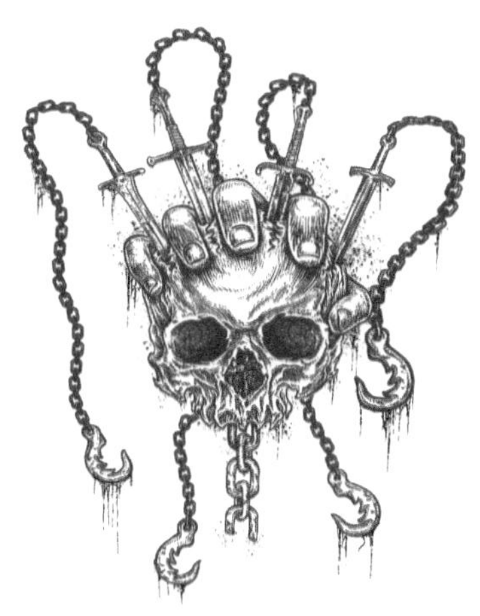

CHAPTER SEVEN
TOWN OF ENDWYN

Darius returned to the bakery just after dark. Gunvald and Bear were sitting at a small wooden table in the corner of the front room, talking and drinking beer.

"Figures," Darius said with an eye roll. "I do all the hard work and you guys sit around drinking."

"I take it you found a way through?" Gunvald asked, but the smug expression on Darius's face already gave away the answer.

"When have I ever let you down?" Darius said, puffing out his chest.

"There was that time in Edgehelm," Gunvald said.

"And Hollowell, when you used that ring we were supposed to deliver to that noble's wife as a bottle opener and left it in the tavern," Bear added.

"The brothel in Frostmoor," Gunvald added.

Bear bobbed his head. "Frostmoor was a shitshow. Literally."

"Fuck you guys," Darius said. "And you weren't even at Frostmoor, Bear, so what are you talking about?"

"I heard about it, though," Bear said with a nod. "From several people, actually."

Darius sighed.

"So what did you find?" Gunvald asked.

"There's a slave caravan headed for Krul coming through here tomorrow morning. Apparently, they lost some guys in a bandit attack and need some new muscle."

"Wouldn't be the first time we took a caravan job," Bear said.

"Who's caravan?" Gunvald asked.

"Morrow."

"Figures, it would be that asshole," Bear said.

"Krul only gets us through one checkpoint,

though," Gunvald said.

"Yeah," Bear said, "but the safest way out of the wastelands from Krul would be to head north through the second checkpoint and into Hollowell. Even an asshole like Morrow knows that."

Gunvald nodded. "So, who attacked the caravan?"

"Word is it was a group of Cleansers," Darius said, grabbing a bottle of beer from the table. He took a seat in an empty chair.

"Cleansers?" Bear scoffed. "Those fucking guys are worse than slavers."

Gunvald hadn't heard of the Cleansers, but he had more than his fair share of dealing with slavers. All of them being self-absorbed assholes with a superiority complex that rivaled most nobles. "That a new faction or something?"

"Basically a cult of retired mercs and wannabe knights," Bear said. "They go after unsanctioned magic users under the guise of preventing another Ten Year War."

"What kind of unsanctioned magic?" Gunvald asked.

"Anything that isn't taught in the Tower," Darius said. "You really haven't heard about this shit?"

"I've been kinda busy killing people," Gunvald replied.

Bear said, "I heard they recently tore up Terrin looking for a young girl they claimed was a Channeler."

"There hasn't been a Channeler on Anezen in at least half a century," Gunvald said.

"I don't know." Bear took a swig from his beer bottle and set it down on the table. "But they have King Barramore's blessing, so you better watch that sweet ass of yours, D. You're not exactly slinging Tower magic around."

"Fuck that. Let 'em come," Darius said. He drew his mage cannons and spun them. "I'll introduce them to my new friends here."

"Are you still going on about those things?" Bear asked. "You know, if you want some help jerking off to your new toys later, my door is always open."

"Alright. That's enough of you assholes for tonight. I see where this conversations going." Darius stood up and stuffed the guns back in their holsters. He grabbed his beer bottle. "If you need me, I'll be at the inn."

"Aw, come on, D, I've got plenty of room here," Bear said, gesturing around the bakery.

"Nope. Not a chance. I said my piece and now

I'm out." He grabbed one of the few leftover loaves of bread that were still sitting on the table by the door and shoved them under his arm. "This shit's too good to let it go to waste." Then he left.

"Do you really have to do that?" Gunvald asked, wrapping his hand around his almost empty beer bottle.

"Trust me, Gunvald, I have a sixth sense for these things. He's definitely playing for both sides; he just doesn't realize it yet." Bear smiled. "The real question is, do *you* really have to do *this*?"

Gunvald gazed at his beer bottle and didn't say anything. He knew he was risking their lives, not to mention breaking their morals, but what had to be done, had to be done. He wasn't going to let the best chance they had to kill Amaya slip away, no matter the cost.

"Look, I wouldn't be here today if you hadn't pulled my ass outta Dunstead," Bear said. "I'm a man who pays his debts. So if this is what we gotta to do to pay that bitch back for what she did to Leanna and your boy, then we do it, no matter how fucked up it is. But sneaking into Driftmoor Castle is gonna be hard enough in itself, and then killing Adder's daughter. Adder's family. You don't see the hypocrisy in that?"

Gunvald gulped his beer. Of course he could see

it. A fucking blind man could see it. But it was the only way to lure Amaya out.

"I don't have a choice."

"The fuck you don't." Bear shook his head. "Leanna would not have wanted this, and you know that."

Gunvald slammed his fist on the table. "She's dead, Bear. It doesn't matter what she would want."

"And that makes it okay to kill a kid?"

"Nothing makes it 'okay,' but it is what it is. I've killed enough people in the past three years to fill a fucking city trying to lure her out, and I've got shit to show for it. This is the only way she's gonna show."

The two men sat in silence for a minute. Then another. Then Bear sighed. "Are you sure his kid can do what you say she can?"

"I've seen her do it," Gunvald said. "Brought a fucking dead dog back to life. But it wasn't right. The spirit wasn't fully reattached to its body, but I'm guessing that'll change once her magic awakens."

"And how long until that happens?"

"She turns thirteen in a week," Gunvald answered.

"That's cutting it close."

It was, but Gunvald's plan revolved around

pissing Amaya off enough to show herself. And killing Ceres before Amaya could get her hands on her would do just that.

Gunvald shrugged. "Well, if somebody hadn't gotten themselves thrown into Whitestone..."

"And if Amaya already knows about her?"

"The only way she would know was if she was in the area when Ceres used magic, or when she awakens, and I'm sure I wouldn't have gotten as close to Ceres as I did if she already knew."

Bear paused to drink his beer. "Well, fuck us then, huh?"

"Yeah," Gunvald finished off his beer. "Listen, I'm tired. I'm going to bed." He got up from the table and walked into the back room of the bakery, leaving Bear fiddling around with an empty beer bottle.

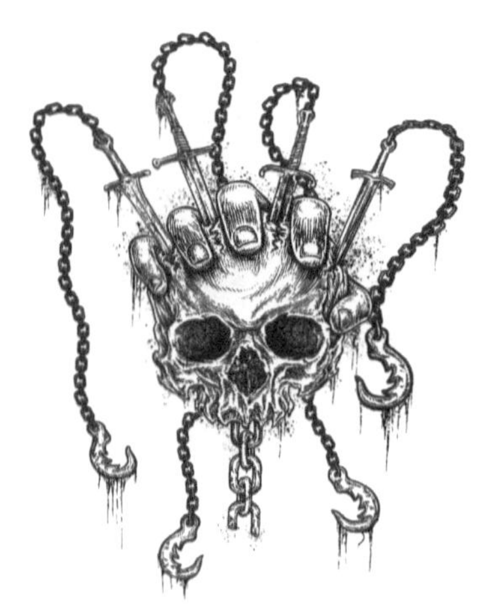

CHAPTER EIGHT
TOWN OF ENDWYN

Gunvald couldn't sleep. He tossed and turned and sweated; he even tried counting sheep, but nothing worked. His conversation with Bear had brought up memories he had fought to keep buried. Memories of Amaya. Memories of his family.

He thought about it every time he shut his eyes, like an unending fucking nightmare.

It was three years ago. Gunvald, Bear, and Darius had been drinking away the loss of their friend, Pavel, who had been killed during their last spirit collection. A collection involving the two men responsible for the destruction of Gunvald's village, and the murder of his parents, and Gunvald had made sure they paid for it.

It was late, and Gunvald had just stumbled home. Leanna and his son Egil were fast asleep. He had no sooner made it to the living room when someone knocked lightly on the door.

He sighed and opened it. Amaya was standing there with four of the town guards.

"Thank you, boys, for a lovely evening," she told the guards, rubbing one on the cheek playfully.

Gunvald walked back into the living area and waited.

Amaya followed him inside and closed the door.

"What was that about?" Gunvald asked.

"Just killing some time," she said. "You're out late."

She walked over to the kitchen table and waved her hand. The four boxes that had previously held Gunvald's swords appeared. Gunvald stepped towards the table, placed each sword in their respective boxes and closed the lids. Amaya waved her hand, and the boxes disappeared.

"Are we finally finished?" Gunvald took off his boots and tossed them in the corner.

"Almost. The spirits you delivered. Did you rend them from the bodies?"

"You know damn well what happened to them."

"Those spirits are useless to me," Amaya said.

"What did you fucking expect?"

"I expected you to be professional."

"You knew exactly what would happen when you sent us after them. Don't give me that bullshit." Gunvald got in Amaya's face. "Our contract was for twenty spirits, and that's what I fucking delivered. Bringing them to you undamaged was a courtesy, not a requirement."

"It was expected," Amaya snapped. "Rendered spirits are useless. You know this. So as far as I'm concerned, you still owe me two spirits."

"And as far as I'm concerned, I don't give a shit," Gunvald said. "Pavel's dead, and I'm done. Now, can you kindly fuck off so I can go to bed?"

"I'm gonna ask you nicely, Gunvald. One more time," Amaya said sweetly. "I promise these two will be easy. So easy you won't even need your men. Then you will be done."

"And I already told you to fuck off. We're done, Amaya."

"I see. That's a shame."

Gunvald heard footsteps coming down the stairs. Egil stepped into the living room, rubbing his eyes. "Dad? What's going on?"

"Nothing, go back to bed," Gunvald said.

"Who are you?" Egil asked Amaya.

"She's just a friend," Gunvald said, trying to hide his anger. "Now go back to bed. I'll be up in a minute."

The front door slammed open, and the four guards stomped into the room. They grabbed Gunvald's arms and forced him to his knees.

"Get the fuck off me." Gunvald struggled, but they were much stronger than he expected. Much stronger than they should have been.

"Dad!" Egil swatted one of the guards on the arm, but the guard didn't seem to notice.

Amaya grabbed Egil by the back of the neck and lifted him into the air.

"Let him go!" Gunvald yelled. He threw an elbow back into the crotch of a guard, but the man didn't move or make a sound.

"It didn't have to be this way, Gunvald." She held Egil in the air. The boy kicked and screamed to no avail. "All you had to do was agree to collect two more spirits."

Leanna ran down the stairs and straight at Amaya. "Put him down!"

Amaya backhanded her in the face with a loud smack. Leanna fell to the floor in front of Gunvald, her neck twisted at a crooked angle.

Gunvald kicked and twisted, but the guards just gripped him tighter.

"I'm sorry, Gunvald." Amaya slammed Egil's head against the wall. Egil screamed.

Gunvald tried to stand, but a guard kicked his legs out. "You fucking witch!"

"I tried, Gunvald." She slammed Egil's head against the wall again. Blood poured from his nose. "I tried to resolve this." She slammed his head against the wall again. "I was being nice." She slammed his head once more and he stopped screaming. She dropped him onto the floor.

Chunks of blood and brain dripped down the wall.

"Now, you can consider our contract fulfilled."

Amaya knelt down and helped the spirits of Leanna and Egil to their feet, then she wrapped her hands around their necks.

Gunvald screamed.

Four swirling black holes appeared in the air. A

thick black chain streamed out of each one. One of the chains smashed straight through the head of one guard; another through a guard's neck. Both men toppled stiffly to the floor. Then, covered in blood and brain matter, they wrapped themselves around Gunvald's torso. The other two chains wrapped around each of Gunvald's arms.

Then, the four swords came out of the holes. Dimittis and Obitus sliced the heads off the two remaining guards, spraying blood and gore into the air, and slid into Gunvald's hands. The other two swords landed on the floor behind him.

"How?" Amaya stared down at him.

Gunvald lunged at Amaya, but she disappeared into thin air, taking the spirits of Leanna and Egil with her.

Gunvald didn't remember how many other guards he had killed that night, but he remembered it took five guards as well as Olin and Bear to subdue him.

Gunvald thought he had buried that memory for good.

He got out of bed and wiped the sweat off his face using a small towel and basin Bear had left in his room. There was no sense in trying to sleep anymore. Once the nightmares started, they never ended, plus it was almost light, and they had a slave caravan to catch.

* * *

Gunvald, Bear, and Darius waited at the twin bridge crossroads. The air was chill, and dark clouds threatened rain. Their horses grazed leisurely on a small patch of grass on the side of the road.

Bear leaned heavily on his massive war mallet. Despite its six-foot shaft and barrel-sized steel head, it looked small next to him. "So who'd you steal the sword from?"

"Why is that the first thing you assume?" Darius unsheathed a pristine short sword. It had a braided silk grip, engraved cross-guard, and the image of a bear carved into the pommel. "Maybe I just found it lying around; you don't know. Besides, it reminded me of you."

"Uh huh."

"What?" Darius shrugged. "It's got a good heft to it." Darius twirled the sword a few times with his wrist before sheathing it. "And I lost my old one when I got thrown into Whitestone."

"And why was that again?" Bear asked.

"Nice try, but it'll be a cold day in Helios before

you get that one outta me."

Gunvald asked. "These Cleansers you mentioned last night. Silver armor, white half-shoulder capes?"

"Yeah, why?" Darius asked, turning to look over his shoulder. "Aw, shit."

Five Cleansers were riding toward them, a cloud of dust pluming behind them.

Bear hefted his mallet. "It only took one day for you to get us in trouble, D. That's gotta be a record."

"Oh, fuck off."

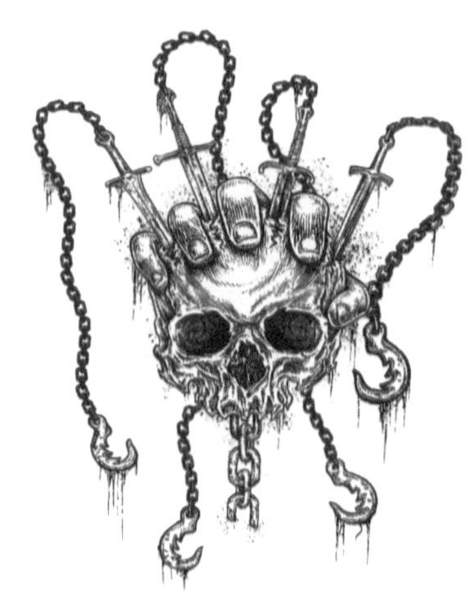

CHAPTER NINE
THE TWIN BRIDGE CROSSROADS

The Cleansers rode up and surrounded them. One, just a hair taller than Gunvald, dismounted and walked up to Gunvald, removing his barbute and donning a large smile. A deep scar etched its way from the top left side of his forehead, cutting across his nose and down his right cheek, disappearing into a thick, untamed beard. "If I'd known there was going to be a reunion, I would have brought cookies."

That bastard Hargraves was the last person Gunvald would have guessed to be under that helmet.

Darius stepped forward and spat at Hargraves's feet. "The only reunion you need is with Amaya."

"Hargraves," Gunvald said, putting his hand on Darius's chest to keep him from getting into the man's face.

"Gunvald," Hargraves replied. "It's been a while."

"So, this is your new outfit?"

"What can I say? The good King pays well. And the benefits—" Hargraves smiled. "—are simply too good to resist."

Bear chimed in, "If Barramore is hiring shits like you, it's no wonder the Cleansers have the reputation they do."

Hargraves dismissed the insult with a wave. "You think I give a shit about reputation? Please... But anyway, enough about me. What brings you fine gentlemen out to this barren paradise?"

"Just resting the horses," Gunvald said.

"Are you, now?" Hargraves raised an eyebrow. The other four Cleansers dismounted. "You're a hard man to miss, Gunvald, especially with those things dragging behind you."

"Meaning?"

"Meaning I know you've already been to

Endwyn. I also know that any minute now a slave caravan will pass through here, headed to the wastelands. You wouldn't know anything about that, would you?"

His swords began whispering their way into Gunvald's thoughts, urging him to gut Hargraves right where he stood. He could feel the chain connected to Obitus tighten around his chest, but he urged the sword to stay put. "How about we cut the shit and you just tell me what you want?"

Hargraves glanced at Darius. "I was just here for the slavers, but bringing in Darius Ryker would be a much more lucrative endeavor."

"The fuck does that mean?" Darius asked.

"He gets paid to bring in unsanctioned magic users. Don't you?" Bear said.

Hargraves smiled and shrugged. His mail clattered. "You're as unsanctioned as they get, D."

Darius got up in Hargraves's face. "You want unsanctioned? How about an unsanctioned hole in your fucking forehead?" He drew a mage cannon from his right holster and held it up to Hargraves's scarred nose. Gunvald thought Darius might actually do it, but Darius holstered the gun again.

Hargraves nodded. The other four Cleansers

unsheathed their swords and approached. Their fingers clenched much too tightly around their hilts. They shifted from foot to foot. One of the men's swords was shaking. These men were green.

"I guess it shouldn't be a surprise you'd be willing to throw away four of your men's lives for a chance at a bit of coin," Gunvald said.

Bear swung his leg behind a Cleanser's leg and tripped him onto his back. Then he raised his mallet and slammed it down on the man's chest, leaving a massive dent in the man's chest plate. The Cleanser gasped for breath as Bear slammed the mallet into the Cleansers face.

One Cleanser swung his sword at Darius. Darius blocked it with his short sword, pulled out his mage cannon with his other hand, and fired it into the eye slit of the Cleanser's helmet.

The Cleanser dropped his sword and tore off his helmet. His right eye socket was a gaping, burning, bloody hole.

Hargraves swung his sword at Gunvald. Gunvald raised his hand, knowing one of his swords would be there. It was Cinis. Their blades locked together. Hargraves gritted his teeth and pushed. Gunvald twisted his wrist, broke the lock, and punched

Hargraves in the face.

Hargraves stumbled backward. Gunvald swung for Hargraves's throat, but Hargraves spun away from the strike and stepped back. "You're losing your edge, Gunvald."

Hargraves seemed to look over Gunvald's shoulder. His eye twitched. The Cleanser behind Gunvald swung wildly. Obitus moved on its own and parried the blow with a loud clash of metal, and Dimittis plunged itself below the Cleanser's helmet and into his neck.

Hargraves lunged forward and thrust his sword at Gunvald's chest. Gunvald sidestepped it and stabbed Cinis at Hargraves's groin. Hargraves deflected the strike and again launched himself at Gunvald.

Obitus shot forward, again of its own volition, and stabbed Hargraves's left leg just below his armor. Hargraves grunted and fell to a knee.

Darius skewered another Cleanser with his short sword, then turned to Hargraves, spat in the man's face, and pressed the mage cannon's barrel to his head. "What now, asshole?"

Gunvald tossed his swords on the ground. "Why, Hargraves?"

"Why, what?"

Darius screamed at him. "What do you mean, why what? Dunstead? Fucking setting us up?"

"Fuck you, that's why," Hargraves growled. "Go ahead, kill me. See what happe–"

Darius fired the spell pistol. The firebolt burned through the side of Hargrave's head. Hargraves groaned. The pungent smell of boiling brains wafted from his ears as he fell forward on his face.

"So much for getting answers," Gunvald said.

"I told him I would kill him next time I saw him," Darius said and slid the cannon into its holster.

Bear said, "I wouldn't have pegged Hargraves as a Cleanser."

"Why not?" Darius said. "Joining a crazy cult that gets to do whatever the hell they want because they've got the king's blessing is completely on brand for that fucking piece of shit."

"Maybe. But what were the odds that he was with the first Cleanser we ran into?" Bear asked.

"Probably keeping tabs on us," Gunvald said. "I wasn't exactly subtle in Breham."

"Are you ever?" Bear asked. "But we have to assume he isn't the only one looking for Darius."

"Fuck 'em!" Darius said, pulling the still smoking mage cannon out of its holster and twirling it around his fingers. "Let them come." He waved the gun at Gunvald's swords. "But, you do kinda stand out, what with the chain swords and shit."

Bear asked, "Speaking of swords, since when can you move them around like that?"

"I can't," Gunvald said.

"What do you mean, you can't?"

"Exactly that."

"Wait, wait, wait." Darius looked nervous. "Are you saying those freaky-ass swords are now stabbing people on their own?"

"You saw what you saw," Gunvald told him.

Bear stared down at the blades lying on the dirt road. "A little warning would have been nice. That's not something you keep to yourself. How long has this been going on?"

"Since Whitestone."

Darius narrowed his eyes at Gunvald. "You coulda mentioned that. I'm not lookin to get stabbed in my sleep because your swords just randomly get the urge to kill someone."

"I've got it under control," Gunvald said.

Bear and Darius exchanged glances.

Darius shook his head. "I hope so."

Their concern was more than justified. The

swords gave Gunvald no indication, no whispers, nothing to let him know when they were going to act. He wondered if he could even stop them if they did. It would be a lie to say that he wasn't also concerned, but he had to trust that they would only lash out at his enemies.

"Our ride is here," Bear said, nodding his head towards a large, wobbly cart trundling toward them.

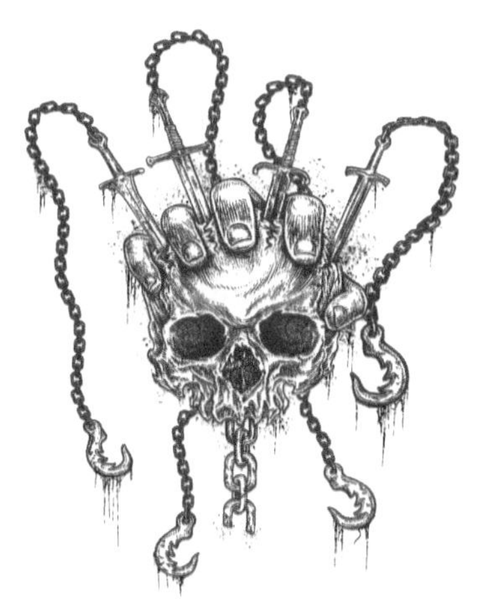

CHAPTER TEN
TOWN OF DUNSTEAD
EIGHT YEARS EARLIER

It was just past midnight. Gunvald, Darius, and Hargraves crept around a small stone house. Two houses stood between them and the trolls' new leader, the Grul'Dak, Ozug.

"I don't like this," Darius whispered. "It's too quiet."

"Relax, we're good," Hargraves said with a wave of his hand. "Besides, we got Pavel and Bear watching our backs. We're good."

Darius muttered. "For now."

Gunvald had no idea why the Krul trolls decided to attack Dunstead, or why Amaya wanted their new leader's spirit. All he knew was that it was too quiet for a town being torn apart by trolls.

"You said there were three trolls with Ozug, so where are they?" Darius asked.

"Maybe they're out taking a piss, how the fuck should I know?" Hargraves said.

Gunvald waved them forward. They crept behind the next house. The full moon made it easy to avoid falling on their faces.

"Any eyes on them?" Gunvald asked. Darius and Hargraves shook their heads. "If they're inside, we're gonna be in the shit. That house is too small to fight three trolls in."

"An extra troll or two won't make a difference," Hargraves said, pulling his sword from its sheath.

They stepped quietly to the back of the next house. Darius and Hargraves pressed themselves against the wall on either side of the wooden back door. Gunvald put his ear to the door. Nothing.

"You sure this is the house?" Gunvald whispered.

Hargraves nodded.

Gunvald slowly pushed the door open. Its

hinges creaked long and loud.

The house's interior was dimly lit by the flickering flames of a fire in the fireplace, making the air thick with the faint smell of smoke. The back hallway was barely wide enough for Gunvald's shoulders, but the living area was surprisingly spacious.

Darius silently slipped into the room behind Gunvald, spell pistol in hand. Hargraves was lagging behind. Gunvald waved a hand at him to hurry the hell up, but Hargraves just shrugged. Darius tapped Gunvald on the shoulder and pointed to a narrow stone stairway leading to the second floor. Gunvald nodded.

They crept silently up the sturdy stone stairs, Darius leading the way. He peeked around the corner at the top of the stairs and whispered, "Clear."

"What do you mean, 'clear'?" Gunvald turned to tell Hargraves, only to find the staircase behind him empty, and the front door on the other side of the living area slightly ajar. Hargraves was nowhere in sight. "The fucker set us up."

"What?" Darius asked.

A guttural voice yelled from outside the house. "Hand of Death!"

Gunvald shoved past Darius and stormed over to a second-floor window. About twenty trolls had surrounded the house. Their leader Ozug, with a jagged bone crown on his head and a rotted-toothed smile stretching across his bulbous face, stood next to Hargraves.

Ozug growled, "Come, let us talk like men."

Darius walked over to the other small window and peered out. "Hargraves! You fucker."

Hargraves smiled. "It's just business. Nothing personal."

Darius spat out the window. "I swear to Fiarus, Hargraves, the next time I see you, your brains are gonna be leaking out of your fucking head."

Hargraves looked around at the throng of trolls. "Somehow I don't think we'll be seeing each other again. Unless my friends here decide to send me your eyes."

Darius pulled his head inside and gritted his teeth. "So what's the plan, Gunvald?"

"We talk."

"No, for real. What's the plan?"

Gunvald ignored Darius and headed towards the stairs. They were well and truly fucked. All they could do was try to get out of there alive.

As he approached the door, Gunvald's swords began a ghostly chorus in his head.

Blood. Death.

Gunvald had never heard them so loud.

"You sure about this?" Darius asked, coming up behind him.

"No," Gunvald said.

He pulled open the front door and stepped outside.

The number of trolls around the house was probably twice what Gunvald had seen out the window, and the stink almost swept him away. His heart was racing, the swords were raging in his mind, and he was sweating like a grill chef.

Ozug grunted. "Hand of Death, we finally meet." His lips were crusted with blood.

Gunvald walked past him toward Hargraves.

"Don't look at me like that, Gunvald," Hargraves said. "Like I said, it's just business."

Ozug grabbed Gunvald's arm and spun him around to face him. "He is not your concern, Hand of Death. I am."

"Fine," Gunvald said.

Gunvald drew Obitus from its scabbard, and thrust the broken, jagged blade up through Ozug's chin and into his skull. Thick green blood, like swamp water in both look and smell, gushed over Gunvald's hand. He ripped the sword back out.

Ozug fell onto the dirt with a heavy thud.

"Shit," Gunvald realized he hadn't given the move much thought. He looked at the bloody, green half-sword and could have sworn it laughed at him.

The other trolls drew their crude weapons and charged him.

Gunvald dropped Obitus and drew the hand-and-a-half sword Cinis from the scabbard on his waist. Its hilt pulsed in his hands.

Yes. Blood.

A wild-eyed troll swung a poleaxe down at Gunvald. Cinis rose up and severed the troll's arm at the elbow. A second troll, thick and fat, lunged at Gunvald. It raised its monstrous club, and an arrow pierced its left eye. It howled, dropped the club, and grabbed its face. Gunvald jammed his sword into its stomach, its entrails spilling onto the dirt.

Another troll charged Gunvald, but two arrows to the neck dropped it to the ground. Gunvald glanced around. Pavel was perched precariously on the adjacent rooftop, reloading.

Two trolls stepped toward Gunvald. He gripped Cinis tight with both hands, trying to plan a move. Then the ground trembled, and Bear, ten-feet tall in his bear form, smashed through the trolls, teeth bared in a furious snarl, knocking them both to the ground.

"Thanks," Gunvald told him. He glanced around.

Two massive trolgres, grotesque blends of troll and ogre, had gathered at the corner of the adjacent house and were pulling stones from it with their enormous fists, trying to knock it down and get at Pavel. He couldn't see Darius anywhere. "Darius! Go help Pavel!"

Darius yelled, "Fuck!" from somewhere behind him. Gunvald wasn't sure if that meant he needed help or he didn't want to help Pavel. Either way, he was in no position to find out.

Gunvald plunged Cinis through the chest of an attacking troll. "Bear! We need to get the fuck out of here!"

Bear roared, nodded his massive brown head, and clawed the face off an approaching troll. Bear pushed through the trolls. Some backed away from him; others he had to throw. Then, a thrown spear pierced his left hind leg.

Bear roared. Another troll jumped on his back and swung a battered cleaver down onto his flank. Bear stumbled to all fours.

"Bear!" Gunvald grabbed the chain connected to Iudicium, twirled it above his head, loosened his grip, and stuck the chains hook into the troll's neck. He yanked the chain and tore a gaping gash in the creature's neck. The troll frantically sucking air through the hole before it collapsed.

Gunvald stood over Bear. The trolls formed a circle around them, grunting and growling. He called Dimittis and Obitus into his hands.

He whispered to Bear, "Change back."

If he had to carry his friend out of there, it would be much easier if Bear were human.

Bear began breathing heavily. He groaned. Then he turned his giant head to look at Gunvald. "Just go," he growled.

Gunvald shook his head. "Not a chance."

"Don't be stupid," Bear growled. "Go!"

Gunvald ignored him. If they were going to die here, he would carve a pile of troll heads and limbs before he faced Amaya one last time. The swords, perhaps sensing his thoughts, began to whisper...

Blood. Death. Kill.

"Shut up," Gunvald said.

They didn't listen. Their incessant whispering only grew louder until he could barely hear himself think.

"You want blood?" Gunvald muttered. "Then stop your whining and help me get it!"

The swords' whispering swelled into a roar, like a storm blowing through a canyon. A burning sensation flowed through him. His vision shrunk to a pinpoint, and his body moved on its own. He realized he wanted blood as much as they did, maybe more so…

* * *

"Come on, Gun, snap out of it."

"Darius?"

It was morning. The sunlight stung Gunvald's eyes and his mouth was full of dust. He spat some out and wiped his tongue on his dusty forearm, which didn't help. He rubbed his eyes and saw that Pavel and Darius were standing over him.

"What the fuck happened?"

"From what I can tell," Darius told him, "you single-handedly slaughtered an army of fucking trolls."

All Gunvald could remember was feeling trapped in his own body. "Bear?" he asked, scanning the litter of troll corpses.

"Pavel patched him up the best he could, but he needs a real healer."

"Will he make it back?"

"He should," Pavel said. "We can load him onto one of the carts across town. I'm sure there's at least one that's still usable."

"Finally, come to your senses?" It was Amaya's voice. Unforgettable.

Gunvald looked to his left and saw her walking towards him, black dress flowing like a raven's feather.

"She showed up last night out of nowhere and took out the two trolgres." Darius ran a hand through his disheveled hair. "Then she threatened to uh... rend us from existence if we tried to help you."

"What the hell are you talking about?" Gunvald raised his head.

"Yes, dear," she cooed, and brushed his face with the back of her hand. "It seems you weren't quite yourself last night. I know how much it would have pained you to wake up and find that you had slaughtered your friends here in your little rage-induced possession. So I kept them safe." She smiled and leaned in close to Gunvald's ear. "But just between you and me, I really didn't want to have to guide more spirits to the afterlife than I had to."

She stood up and glanced at the corpses strewn over the dirt road. "There you are." She glided, ghostlike, over to Ozug, lying sprawled and still with a big, crusty hole under his chin. She knelt beside him.

Gunvald turned away. He'd seen enough bloodshed for one day. The screams of the dying still echoed in his ears, and the tang of blood filled his nostrils. He just wanted to stand up and get out of there, but his body was having none of it. He raised his arms toward Darius and Pavel. "Help me up."

They pulled his arms up and his legs, still burning with muscle ache, eventually found themselves under him.

Darius reached down to grab his swords.

"Leave them!"

Gunvald fumbled with the scabbard straps, but eventually loosened them and let them fall to the ground. After last night, he didn't want those fucking swords anywhere near him.

CHAPTER ELEVEN
NORTH BRIDGE ROAD

The slave cart wobbled to a stop in front of Gunvald, Darius, and Bear. It was nothing more than a steel cage overflowing with slaves, mostly women, mounted on four wheels and pulled by two worn-out brown horses. Six other men, all in full leather armor, rode alongside the cart. They stopped their horses and stared at Gunvald.

Behind the cart, a thick chain dragged four more male slaves. If Gunvald hadn't just seen them walking, he'd have thought they were corpses.

Morrow Gnash, a short, round man, hopped

down from the cart's driver's seat and approached Gunvald, his messy braided beard swinging with each step. "I see you handled our Cleanser problem. One less thing to worry about." He snatched the whip from his belt and punched it into Darius's chest. "Make yourself useful," Morrow nodded to the back of the cart, "and keep those four in line."

Gunvald took the whip from Darius and threw it back at Morrow.

"We're here to keep your slaves alive, not keep them in line."

Morrow scoffed and picked up the whip. "Useless," he muttered, then stormed back toward his wagon.

"The fuck is his problem?" Darius asked.

"If I had to guess, I'd say it was your skin," Bear said.

For most slavers, slaves were slaves. Age, sex, and skin color didn't matter. The only thing that mattered was whether they could fetch a good price. All the slaves in Morrow's cage, however, as well as the four chained at the back, had dark skin like Darius's.

"Given Morrow's a racist bastard," Bear said, "I'm surprised he hired us in the first place."

"Maybe it was my dazzling personality?" Darius

said.

"Or maybe he hopes to cut a deal with the Cleansers."

"I wouldn't put it past him," Gunvald said. "But either way, we need him to get through the checkpoints, so for now, we treat this like any other job."

"Whatever you say, boss," Darius said.

Gunvald walked towards their horses. His gut was telling him to leave, take the long way to Driftmoor Castle, but they had less than a week before Ceres's powers matured, and he wasn't about to let his last chance at revenge slip away.

* * *

The slave caravan arrived at the first checkpoint around dusk, just as a drizzle of rain started to come down. Gunvald and his men rode at the back of the cart, while the other six men rode three to each side. The checkpoint's tall stone wall went straight to the mountains on either side of the road, completely sealing off the narrow pass. Gunvald counted at least twenty guards stationed on top of it.

What was once a way to manage the wasteland's traffic had since become nothing more than a way for

Adder to fill his purse.

Beyond the checkpoint lay the cracked and barren ground of the wastelands. An endless stretch of dry, lifeless earth, littered with rocks that jutted from the ground like teeth.

The cart creaked and groaned to the archway, where three guards were standing. The guard at the front, a large man with a bushy mustache, watched with narrowed eyes as Morrow climbed off of the driver's seat and waddled his fat ass towards them.

A white cloth, shimmering like a ghost behind the gate, caught Gunvald's attention.

"Cleansers. Behind the gate."

"You sure?" Darius asked.

"No. But keep your head down just in case."

Darius pulled the hood of his cloak down over his face. "Control those creepy swords, and try not to get us killed."

Gunvald glanced at Morrow's guards. They were all staring at Darius. Shit was about to go south.

"You think it's a setup?" Bear asked.

"Not sure," Gunvald told him. Morrow suddenly seemed to be very friendly with the guard at the front. Gunvald was starting to think it would have been better to have just killed Morrow before they set out and tried to bluff their way through.

Morrow nodded to the guard and headed back to the cart. The guard made a sweeping motion with his hand, and the heavy portcullis groaned upward. Morrow urged the horse forward.

"Be ready," Gunvald whispered, nudging Nomad forward.

Gunvald, Darius, and Bear kept an eye on the checkpoint guards. The clop of hooves and the snorting of horses grew louder as Morrow's six other men rode up just behind them, too close for Gunvald's liking.

Two men in telltale white cloaks were standing just behind the checkpoint gate. Gunvald's swords whispered in his head as soon as he saw them, but he fought them back. He had to keep them from lashing out.

The Cleansers eyed Darius as he rode past, then shifted their gazes to Gunvald, muttering among themselves. One smiled at him.

"Kill them! All of them!"

The swords began roaring in Gunvald's head, even as the Cleansers turned their attention away from Gunvald to the six guards riding behind them.

"You alright?" Bear asked.

The Cleansers turned away and started speaking

with some of the checkpoint guards, and the whispers in Gunvald's head backed off just enough to give him space to speak.

"Yeah, fine."

"This doesn't make sense," Darius whispered to him. "Hargraves said he was there for the slave cart, but these guys just let us through, no questions?"

"We might have gotten more out of Hargraves if you didn't shoot him in the head," Bear said.

"Yeah, alright. That one's on me. But still..." Darius said.

"I think the bigger concern is them coming after Darius," Gunvald said. "We don't know if Hargraves found us himself or someone tipped him off, but Olin did say there were a lot of people looking for him."

"So, what do we do?" Darius asked.

"I'm working on it," Gunvald said.

That was a lie. Gunvald had no fucking idea what to do next. He only saw two Cleansers near the gate, but that didn't mean there weren't more hanging around. And he had a feeling Morrow wouldn't risk his other men to help the Cleansers capture Darius, but there's no doubt they'd get in the way just enough to make the Cleanser's job easier.

Luckily, it didn't look like they were gonna

make a move any time soon, so he figured he had until tonight to come up with a way out of this shit.

* * *

They rode for little over an hour before Morrow called for camp. The rocky terrain was a pain in the ass to travel in the daylight. Doing it at night risked breaking a horse's leg, or worse. And though the trolls in Krul might be courteous when they ripped your head off, the ones that roamed the rest of the wasteland just wanted meat.

Morrow picked a rocky outcrop to camp under. Though far from ideal, it was better than camping out in the open. A small pile of smooth boulders to the left of the outcrop would partially block the harsh wind that scoured the wasteland at night. A boon when a fire would certainly call a band of trolls down to cook you over it.

Morrow wedged the slave cart against the end of the boulders to make an additional barrier against the rising wind. Alive and healthy or dead and broken, the slaves would still fetch coin. Ideally, the trolls in Krul would use the men as slaves and the women as playthings until their spirits were crushed. Then they would eat them.

But then again, they weren't very picky. As long as the slaves arrived in some form or another, Morrow would get his pay.

Gunvald, Darius, and Bear set themselves up across from the slave cart, which left them exposed to the wind, but offered an easier escape should the Cleansers show up. Morrow's guards would run a four-man watch through the night. They didn't trust Gunvald's men to take part.

Gunvald stared out the way they had come, looking for any sign that they might be followed.

"You really think they'll be stupid enough to come at us at night?" Darius asked.

"I've learned not to underestimate a man's stupidity," Gunvald said. "Especially when there's coin involved."

"I don't think anyone's stupid enough to risk becoming troll food for a little coin."

"You'd be surprised," Gunvald said. "We'll set up our own watch tonight. Just keep the horses ready in case shit goes sideways."

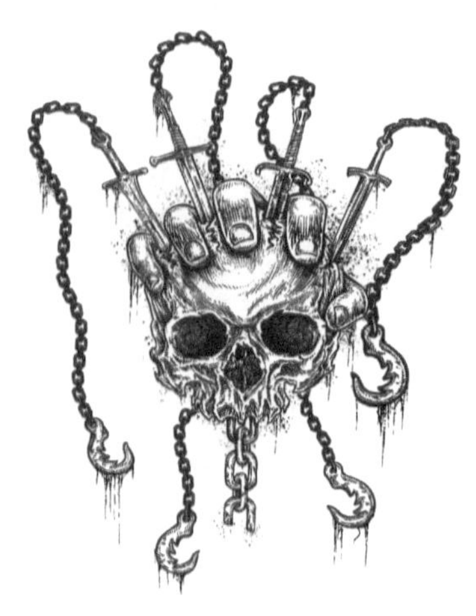

CHAPTER TWELVE
THE WASTELANDS

"Gunvald." Darius shook him roughly. "We've got company."

Gunvald rubbed his eyes and propped himself up on his elbow. Morrow and five of his guards were still sleeping under the outcrop. A torch was flickering on the other side of the slave cart, along with what sounded like several people talking.

"How many?" Gunvald stood with a grunt and nudged Bear with his boot.

"Not sure," Darius said. "But they're gonna get us all fucking killed."

"Stupid…" Gunvald muttered and stormed toward the cart.

"So much for a stealthy escape," Bear said. He reached for his mallet and followed Gunvald.

It wasn't the Cleansers that pissed Gunvald off; it was the flicker of the lead Cleanser's torch. The guy's pointed face, clean-cut dirty blond hair, and well-trimmed beard screamed asshole. Gunvald walked up to him and slapped the torch out of his hand. It clattered across the rocks and puffed out.

The other Cleansers reached for their swords, but their leader raised his hand and stopped them.

The three with the scarred faces and the one with the eyepatch looked like they knew their way around a sword. The two younger ones looked barely old enough to be out this late. The last looked like Bears' long-lost brother.

If this came down to a fight, they might be in trouble.

The leader rubbed the hand Gunvald had slapped. "You know that could be construed as assaulting an Officer."

Darius and Bear walked around the slave cart and stood beside Gunvald. The Cleanser smiled.

"Darius Ryker," he said. "We've been looking

for you."

"No shit," Darius spat.

The Cleanser's smile vanished. "It seems like we got off to a poor start. Allow me to introduce myself." The Cleanser extended a hand towards Gunvald. "Captain Voss Calarook."

Gunvald ignored Voss's hand.

Voss cleared his throat. "Yes, well, we only want the gunmage. Hand him over and we'll leave you to your business."

"Hand him over?" Darius said. "You think I'm his property or something? You got a problem with me, tell me to my face."

"Enough," Gunvald said.

"Whatever, man," Darius mumbled.

"I don't give a shit what you want," Gunvald told Captain Voss. "And I sure as fuck don't have time for this shit. Walk away, or don't. It's your choice."

"Is that a threat?" Voss asked. The other Cleansers stiffened up.

"It's a warning. Fuck off."

Gunvald stepped forward as Morrow waddled around the cart, rubbing his eyes. "What's going on here?"

"Like you don't know?" Darius said.

Morrow turned to Gunvald. "It's just business. You know how it is."

"I should fucking gut—"

Something howled in the dark, raw and guttural.

A massive troll leapt from the ledge above them and crashed down on a cleanser, raked open the man's gut and stuffed some offal into its huge maw. The troll turned its head and locked eyes with Gunvald, two feet of intestine hanging from its jagged teeth. Even hunched over the beast stood at least seven-foot tall, all sinew and muscle, arms as long as its legs. It was a lot fucking larger than Gunvald remembered wild trolls being.

Gunvald felt the long hilt of Cinis slide into his hand, and he wrapped his fingers around it. He held it up, gripped it with both hands, and planted his feet. More trolls howled in the distance.

The two young Cleansers charged the beast. Gunvald had to admire their stupidity. The troll whacked the head clean off the first to get there, picked up the other by his upper arm and swung him against the pile of boulders, leaving a splash of blood and bone and bloody white cape.

"Run!" Bear yelled.

Morrow's guards rounded the slave cart.

Gunvald elbowed his way through them. "Get the horses!"

Darius and Bear scrambled to free the horses. A huge troll barreled past Gunvald, shaking the ground beneath his boots, and clawed the eyes right out of a Cleanser's face. The man screamed and collapsed to the ground. Then it picked up one of Morrow's men with both hands and bit his shoulder off.

Gunvald ran to the horses. They were neighing and stomping their hooves. He heaved himself onto Nomad's back and kicked his heels. A troll ran out in front of him. Nomad reared back, almost tossing Gunvald from his saddle. The troll opened its mouth and roared. Gunvald watched in complete astonishment as Obitus flew up and jammed its jagged, broken blade into the beast's mouth and out through the back of its head.

The troll staggered back, collapsed, and tumbled down the rocky slope. Gunvald squeezed Nomad with his heels, and the horse took off. Darius and Bear followed.

"Shit," Darius said, spurring his horse into a run.

Gunvald looked over his shoulder. Two trolls

were lumbering after Darius.

"Deal with them, Darius!" Gunvald yelled.

"Yeah, yeah, yeah," Darius spun around in the saddle, muttered something unintelligible in the noise of the horse's hooves, and raised his hands. A rock wall to their right, which the ledge was on, thundered down in huge boulders and rolled over the trolls.

Darius twisted back around and urged the horse forward with a kick of his heels.

"Since when do you cast without a pistol?" Bear said when Darius caught up with them.

"Some spells are better cast wild."

"That won't slow them down for long," Gunvald said.

"No shit," Darius told him. "That's why you need to get us out of here 'cause we're about to lose the moonlight."

Gunvald glanced up. Dark clouds were moving in. The wastelands were bad enough under a full moon. They were fucked in complete darkness.

Gunvald spun his horse westward. A chill wind whipped his hair across his face.

Darius and Bear exchanged worried glances.

"What are you doing?" Darius asked.

"We're heading to Krul," Gunvald said.

"Why?" Bear asked.

Gunvald glanced over his shoulder. The two pursuing trolls had staggered to their feet. "Wild trolls won't go there."

"For the same reason we shouldn't go there," Darius said. "You know they'll kill us on sight, right?"

"If you have a better idea, then spit it out," Gunvald said.

"Let's go back to the checkpoint and fight our way out. There can't be that many Cleansers left."

"We don't have time to turn back," Gunvald said.

Nomad shrieked and fell, sending Gunvald sprawling.

Darius yelled.

Gunvald scrambled to his feet and looked over his shoulder. Dimittis flew into his hand. Nomad tried to stand, but his fetlock was broken at an ugly angle. "Shit."

Darius wheeled his horse around to Gunvald. "Get on!"

Gunvald dropped Dimittis and grabbed Darius's arm. The horse tensed, but let Gunvald swing himself up. Darius spurred his horse into a run and Gunvald glanced over his shoulder. The two trolls pounced on

Nomad and tore the helpless horse apart.

"Damn it," Gunvald muttered.

Darius looked back. "Gunvald, I'm so—"

"It's fine. Let's go."

CHAPTER THIRTEEN
THE WASTELANDS

The horses made slow progress through the barren, rocky wasteland, giving Gunvald plenty of time to realize how much he missed Nomad.

"Hey, you okay?" Darius asked.

"It's fine," Gunvald grunted.

It wasn't fine, but he didn't feel like talking about it.

Darius looked like he was going to say something more, but decided against it.

Gunvald shook his head. He had bought Nomad three years ago as a birthday gift for his son. He never got a chance to teach Egil how to ride because Amaya had them out on their last collection job the very next day.

It was mid-morning, and Gunvald had led the horse out of the dark, musty stable onto the road. Dimsdale had a reputation built on alcohol and taverns, which the New Year's festivities did nothing to diminish, but most of the townspeople and visitors seemed to still be sleeping it off.

Gunvald welcomed the quiet until Darius shattered it.

"Gunvald!" Darius ran out the front door of his rooming house, his breath puffing out in the cold air.

"You're a little early for New Year's," Gunvald said.

"You didn't think I was gonna miss little man's birthday, did you?" Darius said, passing Gunvald to walk next to the horse. "This for Egil?" Darius patted the horse's neck. "He's gonna love it."

"It is not Egil that I have to convince."

"Wait, you didn't tell Leanna you were buying the horse?"

Gunvald shrugged.

"I know you're new to this marriage thing, Gun, but you always need to ask for permission—that's just how it works." Darius chuckled. "But yeah, you're in trouble, man, and I am so glad I'm here for it."

They walked back to Gunvald's two-story stone house just on the outskirts of the town. Behind the house, enclosed by a wooden fence, lay a field with a small, weathered barn. Gunvald's seven-year-old son, Egil, was swinging a battered wooden practice sword next to it.

"Dad!" Egil yelled. He ran across the field, his shoulder-length black hair, just like Gunvald's own, blowing behind him. "You got a horse!"

Gunvald held the lead out. "No, you've got a horse."

Egil jumped up and down with his fists clenched. "For real?!"

Darius feigned a pout. "I know I can't compete with a magnificent horse like this, but don't I get a hello?"

"Uncle Darius!" Egil yelled and reached over the fence to hug him.

"How've you been, little man?"

"Good," the boy said. Then, he puffed out his chest. "Dad's been teaching me how to use a sword."

"Well, isn't that convenient." Darius drew a black, leather-handled short sword from an equally black leather scabbard. The blade was small, even for a short sword, but its highly polished steel blade shone like a mirror. He handed it to Egil. "Happy birthday, kid."

Egil raised it above his head. "Wow! Dad, look! A real sword!"

Gunvald cast a sidelong glance at Darius. "Seriously?"

Darius shrugged. "It's a harsh world out there, Gun. You know that better than anyone. My man here's gonna need a good sword at his side."

"Darius," Leanna called from the front doorway. "I certainly hope that's your horse Gunvald is holding."

If there ever was such a thing as a shit-eating grin, Darius grinned it. "Oh man, here it comes!"

Leanna walked across the yard, shaking her head, her simple blue dress swaying with each step.

Egil hollered much louder than necessary, as kids do, "Mom! Dad got me a horse! And look!" He swung the sword. "Uncle Darius got me a sword!"

Darius laughed. "Sold out by your own kid."

Leanna stopped next to the men and leaned on the fence. "I thought we were gonna talk about the horse thing?"

"Leanna!" Darius pulled her into a hug and

kissed her cheek lightly. "How've you been? You look great. Love the blue—"

"It's a housework dress, you dimwit," Leanna said, returning the hug. "And you're not gonna sweet-talk him outta this one."

Darius slapped Gunvald's shoulder. "I tried, but you're on your own, man. C'mon, Egil." Darius plucked the lead from Gunvald's hand and led the horse to the opening in the fence. Then he hoisted Egil onto the horse's broad back. "Your dad's gotta have something in that rickety old barn to brush this guy."

"Darius got him a sword, for fuck's sake," Gunvald blurted.

Darius looked over his shoulder. "I asked permission first."

Leanna nodded. "He did."

"Fucking Darius," Gunvald muttered.

"Well, what's done is done." Leanna reached up, wrapped her arms around Gunvald's neck, and kissed him. "It's okay, I still love you. But you're on dish duty for the next month."

She pulled her arms away and walked towards the road; her dress swirling elegantly... "I have to get to the market before that old crone Colette does. I swear she bribes the vendors to put all the fresh stuff aside for her."

The sound of war horns jolted Gunvald back to the present.

The sun was casting long shadows across the desolate wastelands as they approached the narrow pass to Krul. There were no trolls that Gunvald could see in the pass, but another faint blast of war horns told him the guards had seen them.

Darius said, "You better have a phenomenal plan, Gunvald."

He didn't. He just hoped the Grul'Dak would be willing to talk before putting them on a spit.

As they crested a rocky hill, the gate came into view, two tall, crude wooden doors. A company of armed trolls were waiting impatiently. The trolls of Krul were slightly shorter and thicker than the wild trolls, but no less powerful. They were still all sinew and muscle, except their bodies were much more proportionate to that of a human. A very large, angry human.

Gunvald slid from the back of Darius's horse, swords clattering to the hard-packed earth. He assumed the Grul'Dak, the trolls' leader, was the one at the front wearing the chaotic array of clashing armor and a jagged bone crown on his head similar to the one Ozug wore before Obitus split his brain in half.

The troll smiled a jagged, yellow-toothed smile, and came out to meet Gunvald. "Hand of Death," he rasped.

"I'm guessing you're the new Grul'Dak?" Gunvald said.

"Thanks to you," the Grul'Dak said, his native language pushing against his common speech.

Another troll stepped up next to the Grul'Dak, his face smeared with red war paint, and he was missing half of his left lower tusk. "I will gut him where he stands."

"I'll melt your insides before that happens," Darius said, approaching Gunvald from the left, with his mage cannon pointed at the troll's chest.

"No," the Grul'Dak snarled, and shoved the other troll backward.

The war-painted troll growled at the Grul'Dak, spittle flying in the leader's face.

They spoke in the clicks and growls of the trollish tongue. Gunvald couldn't make out any of it. The face-painted troll eventually backed off, and the Grul'Dak turned back to Gunvald. "We have met before, Hand of Death."

"Have we?"

The Grul'Dak stared at Gunvald, cold and hard. "I was there when you drove your sword through my father's skull, but as you can see, it benefited me. So for that, I shall let you speak your last words."

"I demand a skrall," Gunvald said.

All the trolls laughed, a harsh, grating sound like rocks tumbling down a mountain.

"Stupid human," the war-painted troll snarled. He turned to the Grul'Dak. "I will tear his face from his skull."

"By troll law," Gunvald said over them, "you cannot refuse a challenge of skrall."

Gunvald had no fucking idea if that was true. It was just something he had heard from a drunk old man at some dingy tavern in Westham.

"That is troll law," the war troll spat and stepped forward. "You are not troll."

The Grul'Dak yelled at the war troll again, and the war troll reluctantly backed down, again. The Grul'Dak turned to Gunvald.

"What are your conditions?"

"Cleansers occupy the northern checkpoint. I need your help to get past them."

"Bah," the Grul'Dak spat a green glob on the dusty ground. "We have no ties to white cloaks."

"But you have ties to Morrow, the slave master," Gunvald said.

"What about him?"

"The Cleansers led a pack of wild trolls to Morrow's slave cart last night. Your shipment's now in their stomachs."

The Grul'Dak's face contorted, and a guttural growl rumbled from his cracked lips. "Why should I believe you?"

"Because I wouldn't step foot anywhere near this shithole otherwise."

The Grul'Dak huffed loudly. "And when you die?"

Gunvald waved a hand at Bear and Darius. "Then you get them."

Darius opened his mouth to speak, but the Grul'Dak spoke first. "I agree to your terms."

The Grul'Dak smiled, the other trolls roared. It was hard to tell, but Gunvald was pretty sure they were angry. He waited to see of any if them would speak against the Grul'Dak, but none did. Not even the scowling war troll.

Darius whispered in Gunvald's ear, "I hope you know what you're doing."

CHAPTER FOURTEEN
CITY OF KRUL

The stench of troll sweat stung Gunvald's nostrils as the Grul'Dak, flanked by two trolls in mismatched, dented armor, led him, Darius, and Bear like condemned prisoners through the city's narrow alleyways. The face-painted war troll trailed behind them, grunting and muttering something in the trollish tongue.

Small rock-slab houses lined the crude streets of Krul. Behind them were rock cliffs with dark cave entrances. The troll company, which had looked to be on the verge of ignoring the Grul'Dak's agreement and having the men for lunch, vanished when they entered the city. No doubt looking to get the best seat for the Skrall.

"This place is not what I expected," Bear whispered.

"No," Gunvald replied.

Gunvald had never been to Krul; his knowledge of the city was limited to a scattering of unreliable information from unreliable people who told him the trolls lived in garbage pits and ran around naked. So it was no surprise that it was all wrong. Krul's society was far more human-like than he was led to believe.

"Who gives a shit about how it looks?" Darius said. "What you should be worrying about is the fucking skrall thing."

"You don't think Gunvald can beat a single troll in a fight to the death?" Bear asked.

"I don't think we can trust the trolls to keep their end of the deal."

"They will," Gunvald said. "They have no choice."

Darius scowled at him. "You say that now, but the Grul'Dak is the only one who agreed with you. The others didn't seem too thrilled."

At the center of the city, hundreds of trolls were

pressed around a blood-stained pit. The stench of iron and decay hung heavy in the air. The pit's walls, every bit of ten feet high, were slick with blood, and the ground was littered with bones and gore.

As they neared it, four hulking trolls seized Darius and Bear by the arms, while two more disarmed them.

"Get the fuck off me!" Darius struggled against the troll's grip.

A troll shoved Gunvald backwards into the pit. He landed hard on a pile of rotting troll corpses and rolled off onto the jagged rocks. The left side of his head throbbed and blood flowed from a large gash above his eye.

He untangled himself from a knot of rotting intestines and stared up at the Grul'Dak smiling down at him.

"Let the skrall begin!" the Grul'Dak roared. The other trolls howled and thumped their chests.

The largest trolgre Gunvald had ever seen, wearing a ragged loincloth that covered nothing and gripping a massive club in its hand, forced its way through a crowd of trolls, roared, and leaped into the pit.

"What the fuck is this?" Gunvald yelled.

"The skrall is for trolls, which you are not," the Grul'Dak replied. "Fair is fair."

Gunvald's swords raged in his mind.

Blood. Death. Kill.

Gunvald called Cinis, the bastard hand-and-a-half sword, to his hands and conjured the last of his magic. His arms felt like they were on fire, and his skin began to crack like dry earth. Wisps of red mist seeped from the cracks in his arms, and Gunvald could feel his muscles tense and harden to the point he felt they would tear.

The trolgre beat its chest and roared, its ragged teeth bared as a repulsive spray of spittle and phlegm flew in Gunvald's direction. The trolgre charged and swung the club at Gunvald's head. Gunvald sidestepped it, and swung Cinis at the trolgre's side, barely leaving a scratch on the beast's leathery hide. The trolgre swung again. Gunvald rolled under it, got to his feet, and swiped his sword across the trolgre's other flank. Nothing.

The trolgre roared and charged forward, swinging wildly. Gunvald, Cinis mostly, parried the attack, but Gunvald slipped on a greasy bone and nearly fell. The trollgre grabbed the back of Gunvald's head, lifted him into the air, and slammed him on the jagged rocks.

Gunvald screamed. His rapidly depleting powers as a Hand had likely saved him from certain death, but they did nothing to stop the pain. He groaned and tried to scramble to his feet. The trolgre raised its arms and roared at the crowd. Obitus nearly screamed in Gunvald's mind.

Give me blood!

Gunvald summoned the broken blade, charged the trolgre, and plunged Obitus deep into the trolgre's knee. Then he twisted the blade until it was tangled in muscle and cartilage. The trolgre roared and kicked the sword from its leg.

Gunvald threw Obitus between the trolgre's legs and ran around the troll, summoning Obitus into his hand and wrapping the sword's chain around the trolgre's wounded leg. He summoned more magic and pulled on the chain. The trolgre stumbled and fell to the ground.

Gunvald scrambled up the trolgre's body, grabbed onto it's face, and drew the trolgre's spirit into his grasp. The trolgre roared in pain. The trolls around the pit would only see Gunvald pull his hand from the trolgre's face. The tortured spirit in his grasp was for his eyes alone. But the troll's screams were for everyone to enjoy.

Gunvald backed down the trolgre's chest, stuck his hand in the pit at the bottom of the troll's neck and ripped its rib cage open by its sternum, shattering bone and spilling blood and viscera over Gunvald and the jagged rocks. The trolgre's spirit howled as Gunvald squeezed his hand shut, wiping the spirit from existence.

The trolls fell silent. Gunvald locked eyes with the Grul'Dak, who looked on the verge of speaking when the war troll beside the him snarled and leapt into the pit. The Grul'Dak did nothing to stop him. The war troll drew his sword and strode toward Gunvald. The trolls cheered and roared, which sounded pretty much the same.

An intense burning once again ran down Gunvald's arms as he summoned Iudicium to his hand. He swung the sword's chain and plunged the hooked end into the war troll's throat. Then he yanked on the chain and tore out a chunk of meat from the war troll's neck, spraying blood and gore across the pit.

The troll's knees buckled; it gurgled in wet gasps and fell forward on a pile of bones. Gunvald looked up at the Grul'Dak.

The Grul'Dak snarled, waved a hand at Gunvald and turned away from the pit.

A troll dropped a decaying rope ladder down the blood-soaked wall. Gunvald felt weak. Fatigue washed over him, tired, and nauseous. His legs threatened to buckle. He hadn't used that much magic in a long time, and doubted he could again.

The four swords retracted their chains into their pommels until they hung against Gunvald's back. He climbed the ladder slowly. As he neared the top, Darius and Bear extended their hands down to him and heaved him up out of the pit.

The trolls that had gathered to watch the skrall were grunting and growling as they dispersed from the pit's edge.

"Gun, what the hell was that?" Darius asked, wide-eyed.

"A warning," Gunvald breathed. He had barely enough strength to put a voice to his words.

"It was stupid, is what it was," Bear grumbled.

"I had no choice."

"You never do."

Darius turned his back to Gunvald and paced in a small circle. "So what now?"

Two enormous trolls emerged from an alleyway and lumbered toward them, ragged clothes flapping. "The Grul'Dak want you," one growled.

The swords began whispering in his mind—they were never sated—and he was having a hard time quieting them down.

"You alright, Gun?" Bear asked.

"Fine," Gunvald lied.

Bear rolled his eyes, but he didn't press the issue.

The two trolls led them through the streets of Krul, grumbling and muttering between themselves. They passed several trolls who found something else to look at when they spotted Gunvald.

They entered a colossal stone-slab house where the Grul'Dak was standing in the entryway.

"I will honor the outcome of the skrall," the Grul'Dak said. "We will guide you through the mountains, as agreed."

The Grul'Dak stepped close to Gunvald and looked down at him. "But know this, Hand of Death. Once you are through the mountains, the agreement ends, and you are once again meat."

"Fine."

The Grul'Dak snarled. "Get them out of here!"

One of the trolls jerked Gunvald back towards the doorway, almost throwing him off balance. "Move."

Obitus slipped from Gunvald's back and pointed its broken end at the troll's face. Gunvald shouted, "No!"

The other swords' screams filled Gunvald's head.

Kill it!

Gunvald grabbed Obitus by its black hilt and held it by his side. "Just lead the way."

The troll grunted and pushed past Gunvald.

BEAR

CHAPTER FIFTEEN
GRAYMOUNT ROAD

Gunvald had always wondered how so many trolls invaded Dunstead undetected, and now he knew.

The trolls had dug a tunnel from Krul, under the Scarslant Mountains, to just outside of Dunstead. Wide enough for Gunvald, Darius, Bear, their two horses, and their two furious troll escorts, with room to spare.

A large stone slab was blocking the exit, but the two trolls, after much grunting and cursing, were able to slide it to the side. They emerged on a sloping mountainside, just a few feet above the road.

"You are out of wasteland," the troll with a scar over his eye growled. "You are fair game."

Gunvald wanted to laugh.

Dimittis and Obitus shot forward, ripping through the two trolls' necks so fast they didn't have time to grunt.

There were no whispers in Gunvald's mind. No feelings of bloodlust. Just the sound of the troll's corpses tumbling down the mountain onto the road.

Darius gaped at Gunvald. "Please tell me you did that, and not your crazy-ass swords?"

The thought of killing the trolls before they killed him had crossed Gunvald's mind, but he hadn't actually made a decision. "It doesn't matter."

"You know that didn't do us any favors, right?" Darius asked.

"We'll take their heads," Gunvald said. "If there are Cleansers at Driftmoor's gates, we'll play the mercenary card to get in."

Darius scoffed. "You know how much troll blood stinks, right?"

Gunvald raised an eyebrow as if he hadn't been covered in it for a day and a half.

Bear nodded. "Troll heads might be enough to fake the mercenary story, but what are we gonna do about Anezen's most wanted gunmage?"

Gunvald shrugged. "Don't worry, I've got it covered."

"Why do I have bad feeling about this," Darius muttered.

* * *

It was late afternoon when they started passing by some small farms outside of Driftmoor. Gunvald's mind was more focused on the four swords hanging from his back than anything else going on around them. Especially Darius's bitching.

The more he worried about the swords lashing out on their own, the more he started to realize they had always done whatever the hell they wanted. Even when Amaya first presented them to him.

It was roughly ten years ago, Gunvald and his men had just collected the spirit of the Calas burgomaster, Arthur Acot. It was also their first meeting with Darius after saving him from being hanged at the gallows for killing six guards and sleeping with the burgomaster's wife.

They were gathered at a small run-down cabin on the north side of the Terling Forest. The cabin was musty, thanks to its perpetually leaking roof, and branches and leaves grew through the cracks in the wood-plank walls.

The main room had a couple of worn-out chairs and a small wooden table. Two more rooms were in the back, the larger of which contained four rickety beds that looked ready to crumble at the slightest touch; the smaller was a makeshift bar with an assortment of beer and liquor bottles. Bear, Hargraves, and Pavel headed straight there. Gunvald and Darius sat down in the main room.

Gunvald pulled out the soul jar and fidgeted with it.

"So what does Death do with all these spirits you guys collect?" Darius asked.

"She tortures them, then she sends them to the Ashlands."

"Where's that?"

"It's nowhere. It's more like living in a nightmare than a place. A rotting hellscape that makes Helos look like Astrum. The air burns like a sonofabitch just to take a breath and the sky is filled with the ashes of the dead. Spirits sent there get back their physical bodies just so they can be hunted and tortured by demons. And when they die, they're resurrected to begin the cycle again."

"The way you describe it, it's like you've been there."

Amaya had brought Gunvald there years ago, right after his first spirit delivery.

"I'd rather not talk about it."

Hargraves emerged from the back room and propped himself against the door frame. "Hey Gunvald, you—" A knock at the cabin door interrupted him. "Never mind. Hey, new guy, go get the door."

"Me?" Darius looked at Gunvald.

Gunvald nodded.

Darius got up, headed to the door, and grabbed the moldy door handle. Whoever it was knocked again, and Darius almost jumped out of his britches. Hargraves laughed. Pavel and Bear appeared behind him.

Darius took a deep breath and opened the door. Amaya was standing on the other side, her black hair cascading over her shoulders, her dress blending seamlessly with the forest shadows.

She looked Darius in the eyes. "Who are you, darling?"

"I'm... uh... new," Darius stammered.

Amaya smiled. "Hello, New."

Darius grimaced. "I mean, that's not my name. I'm D-Darius Ryker, M-Madam D-Death." He bowed awkwardly.

"You may call me Amaya, Darius Ryker."

"Sure... um... Am-maya." Darius pressed himself against the door and extended his arm to welcome her inside.

"Why, thank you," Amaya said. She sauntered across the room, stopped in front of Gunvald, and reached out her hand. "The rest of you could learn a thing or two from that one."

Gunvald handed her the soul jar. Amaya took the jar, and with her other hand gently traced her fingers along Gunvald's chest. Then she circled the chair and approached Hargraves, Bear, and Pavel, who still lingered in the doorway to the back rooms.

"And do I dare inquire about how many bodies you've left this time?" Amaya asked.

"A couple," Gunvald said. "Maybe a handful."

"A handful, you say?" She grasped Gunvald's left hand and gave him a playful smile. "Twenty-seven bodies is a lot to fit in one hand."

Gunvald glared at Pavel. "Five or six? Fucking hell, Pavel."

Pavel shrugged. "It's messy work."

"No matter," Amaya said, turning back to Gunvald.

Pavel had said his exploding of the tavern only killed a few guards, not twenty-fucking-seven. It wasn't like Amaya to let shit slide, and she had scolded him for less. Something was up. Gunvald had to find out what.

"Now, if you'll excuse us," Amaya said, "I have a few things I'd like to discuss with Gunvald in private."

Pavel laughed, and he and Darius went to the back room. Bear and a sneering Hargraves followed.

Amaya took the seat in front of Gunvald that Darius had been sitting in. She crossed her legs and folded her hands in her lap. "I'll get straight to the point. I want you to be my Hand."

Gunvald hesitated a minute. He was already in pretty deep. "And what would that entail?"

"Nothing more than what you're already doing. Although maybe a tad more difficult." She stood up, strolled to the broken window by the front door, and peered outside.

"What's the catch?"

Amaya spun around and frowned at him. "You wound me, Gunvald. Do you really think I would offer you something with a catch?"

Gunvald grumbled, "No." He hoped it was the

right answer.

"As my Hand, you would also inherit a small portion of my power. You would be stronger, faster, and your stamina..." She approached him, put her hand on his chest, and whispered into his ear. "Your pregnant little barmaid in Dimsdale would be quite impressed, to say the least."

"How do you—"

She dismissed his question with a wave. "Oh, Gunvald, did you think I wouldn't find out?"

It figured she would keep tabs. There wasn't much Amaya didn't know about him, though he'd hoped she wouldn't find out about Leanna.

"Twenty spirits," Amaya said, sitting in front of him again. "You agree to become my Hand, and deliver me twenty spirits. Upon the delivery of the twentieth spirit, I will consider our deal complete, and you'll be free to spend the rest of your life with that adorable little barmaid." Amaya smiled. "And yes, before you ask, I will adequately compensate you and your men for their efforts."

Despite her honesty, there was always a hidden darkness beneath Amaya's seemingly pleasant demeanor. Gunvald had felt it since he first met her. And while he wasn't bound to Amaya, he never felt he could just leave and live his life. Perhaps this was his chance to make a clean break.

"Twenty spirits is a lot," Gunvald said. "After all the ones I've already collected."

"It is."

Gunvald took a few more seconds to mull it over. Amaya never lied—she just didn't tell the whole truth—but if this was his chance to get away from her... "Okay."

"Excellent." Amaya clapped her hands and rose to her feet. "Now that we have that settled, I have something that might make your future gatherings a little less taxing."

She flicked her hand, and four long, thin wooden boxes appeared on the rickety table. With another quick wrist movement, the boxes opened. Each contained a sword with a gleaming blade and an intricately decorated hilt.

First, going left to right, there was a longsword with a black handle and beautifully etched runes on its silver blade. Next was another longsword with a bone-white handle and a distinctive curved blade with a hook at its end. A hand-and-a-half bastard sword was in the next box. Its blade looked rather gray and dull, and its tan leather hilt looked a little too much like human skin.

In the last box was a black-handled castillon with a jagged edge and a broken blade.

"Dimittis, Iudicium, Cinis, and Obitus," Amaya explained. "All forged in the fires of the Ashlands and imbued with the ashes of the dead."

Gunvald stared at the weapons, his palms starting to sweat. "Are they safe?"

"As safe as any sword could be," Amaya said. "Go ahead, pick one up."

Gunvald cautiously stretched out his hand towards Dimittis, the rune-etched longsword. When the tip of his finger brushed its handle, a sudden gust of wind whipped through the cabin, carrying with it the faint scent of rusted metal. Then, a black chain shot out from the sword's pommel and coiled itself around Gunvald's arm. The chain tightened, its end became a pointed hook, and it sunk itself into Gunvald's shoulder.

Gunvald screamed and clawed at the chain. "What the fuck?!"

Amaya gaped at him for a second, then she leaned back into the chair. "The swords form a bond with their owner, imbuing them with their power. But this..." Amaya touched the chain; a spark danced around her hand, and she shook it off. "Well, I guess it likes you... or not."

The hook hurt like a bitch, but it wasn't unbearable. If the sword had the kind of power Amaya said it had, Gunvald would have to put up with it.

"Can you take the chains off them?" Gunvald asked.

Amaya frowned. "Unfortunately, no. At least not on the mortal plane."

"Great," Gunvald muttered.

Suddenly, chains shot out from the pommels of the other three swords and coiled around Gunvald's body. They jolted tight, and their hooked ends dug into Gunvald's back and chest. He howled and crumpled to the floor.

Darius ran into the room and grabbed the hilt of his spell pistol. "What did you do to him!?"

"Whoa! Easy, new guy," Pavel stepped between Darius and Amaya with his hands out. "Let's not do anything stupid."

"What the hell's going on, Amaya?" Hargraves asked.

Amaya winced. "I don't know."

"So fix it," Pavel said.

Amaya tightened her jaw. "I... I can't."

Gunvald groaned and pushed himself up. A rush

of power surged through him, and he almost forgot the hooks digging into his flesh. He heard whispering and looked around. No one was saying anything. "Are these things talking to me?"

Amaya shrugged. "Perhaps."

Blood. Give us blood.

Gunvald whipped around. "Shut up, Pavel!"

The half-elf put up his little hands. "I didn't say anything!"

Feed us blood.

"Gunvald!" Bear said. "You good?"

Gunvald wasn't exactly sure. "Yeah, I think so." The sword's whispers gradually quieted down. "I'm good."

"This is bullshit," Darius grumbled for at least the twelfth time, snapping Gunvald out of his thoughts.

Gunvald wasn't sure if he was bitching about having to ride on the back of Gunvald's horse with a bloody sack of troll heads bouncing on his leg, or that his face was hidden behind a troll's dirty loincloth.

"No, I'm pretty sure it's troll shit," Bear said.

Darius coughed. "Shut up, asshole. Seriously. Let's wrap your face in a fucking trolls diaper and see how you feel."

"I'm not a wanted man," Bear remarked.

"I can't believe neither of you could come up with a better idea than this."

Gunvald said over his shoulder, "You're more than welcome to go back to the wastelands and grab our gear."

"Whatever." Darius gagged. "I think I'm gonna be sick."

Darius leaned to the side and vomited. "Don't worry, I didn't get any on you."

"You better not," Gunvald said.

"I wasn't talking to you. I was talking to the swords."

Bear said, "You're doing a lot of talking for someone who's supposed to be gravely injured."

"Yeah, yeah." Darius gagged again. "Don't worry. I'll probably be dead from the stench before we even get to the gate."

"Speaking of gates," Bear said.

The road turned, and Driftmoor's southern gate came into view. Two guards were leaning against the wall on either side of the steel-barred portcullis.

"I was half expecting Cleansers," Bear said.

Gunvald pushed his horse ahead. "Doesn't mean they're not inside."

Bear nodded as they continued towards the gate.

CHAPTER SIXTEEN
CITY OF DRIFTMOOR

"You still know how to cast a sleep spell, right?" Gunvald asked.

Darius chuckled. "Are you really asking me that?"

"Just have it ready. We can't afford to make a scene if things go south," Gunvald told Darius as they rounded the bend leading up to Driftmoor's southern gate. "And remember, keep your mouth shut."

The guards didn't seem interested in Gunvald until he was right in front of them. His swords' chains were so tight they lay flat under his cloak. They had been silent since they exited the tunnel; now they began whispering for blood.

"Where ya comin from?" the older of the two guards asked.

"Out near Dunstead," Gunvald answered, holding up the bloody sack containing the two troll heads. "A couple of trolls needed dealing with."

He tossed the sack at the guard's feet. The guard scrunched up his nose and turned his head away.

The younger guard waved his pike at Darius. "And what's his deal?"

"A troll ripped—"

Darius leaned over and vomited at the guard's feet. Gunvald tensed and cursed under his breath.

The guard stepped back against the wall. "Aw, come on."

"Troll ripped off half his face," Gunvald said. "He's gonna need a healer."

The guard grimaced and waved them through the gate.

Driftmoor was no Central City, but in terms of livability, it was far better than any other town or city on the northern continent. The streets were clean, no horseshit, cobbles unbroken. The houses were nicely framed wattle-and-daub, clean and bright, some even painted.

Another thing it had going for it over Central City was the absence of holier than thou nobles.

When they were out of view of the guards, Darius ripped the loincloth off of his face. "I swear to all the gods, I'm gonna get both of you back for that shit." He hurled the loincloth into the street.

"So dramatic," Bear said, clapping his hands. "We should look for a theater troupe that needs a clown."

Darius pulled a thread out of his mouth and whipped it off his fingers. "I hate you guys."

Bear chuckled. "So, what's the plan?"

"Find a shitty inn," Gunvald said, "take a bath, storm a castle, and hope we don't fucking die."

Darius whined, "Not much of a plan."

"It's all I've got," Gunvald told him. "You have a better idea?"

Darius didn't answer.

"Then let's find us an inn," Gunvald said.

* * *

Gunvald took a room at the Cunning Head. It was a decent inn. The room had a simple straw-filled mattress, a small wooden table and chair, a small dresser and a chamber pot. The first thing they did was shower and shave, and by dinnertime, they looked like humans again.

"This is so much better," Darius said, rubbing his freshly shaven head.

"I was starting to like the locks." Bear took a seat on the wooden chair in the corner of the room. It creaked under his massive frame.

"Then I'm glad I got rid of them," Darius said.

Gunvald was pacing around the small brown rug in the center of the room.

"So how do we get in?" Bear asked.

Gunvald had been thinking about the best way to sneak into the castle since they entered Driftmoor. He and Bear had done some work for the previous king, King Ranton, shortly before they started collecting spirits for Amaya. He had a few ideas on how to get in, but they were all risky, and they only had until midnight to get to Ceres.

"I was thinking the east side guard tower," Gunvald said. "It's somewhat isolated from the rest of the castle, but without knowing Adder's guard situation, it's a gamble."

"What about cell three?" Bear asked.

Gunvald had completely forgotten about cell three. During the siege of Castle Driftmoor, King Ranton had been using one of the lower store rooms as a makeshift prison, with three crude cells inside.

There were a few times Gunvald and Bear would have to bring the prisoners food. Other than feeding them once a day, the prisoners were mostly ignored.

There was a man named Reeves held in the third cell for months. He had dug a tunnel through the wall trying to escape. He got about three-quarters of the way to the sewer before dying.

With food and supplies running low, Bear thought it best to complete the tunnel as an alternate escape route should the castle fall.

It didn't.

After the siege was over, Bear sealed off both ends of the tunnel, but the tunnel itself was never filled in.

"What's cell three?" Darius asked.

"Long story short, it's a tunnel from the city's sewers to a prison cell in an old storeroom at the bottom of the castle," Bear said.

Darius grimaced and rubbed his bald head. Then he said, "When you say sewers, you don't really mean like…"

"Come on, D. A little piss and shit never hurt anyone," Bear said.

"Yeah, sure," Darius said. "Tell that to everyone in Freyhaven when they had that shit plague a few years ago."

Bear shrugged. "I stand corrected. But it's still our best way to get into the castle."

"I agree," Gunvald said.

Darius sighed and shook his head. "Can we at least eat before we do this?"

"You want to eat before jumping into a sewer? With your weak-ass stomach?" Bear asked.

"Hey, I'm starving."

All they ate in the past twenty-four hours was what little rations they had stashed in their pockets. And they did have a few hours until it was dark, so it wouldn't hurt to get some food in them.

"I could eat," Gunvald said.

"See? Even our fearless leader is hungry," Darius said.

"I didn't say I was against it; I was just looking out for ya," Bear said.

"Yeah, well, I'm all good. So, let's go eat. And you guys are paying for my meal. Least you could do after that loincloth stunt."

Gunvald looked at Bear and then shrugged.

* * *

The Cunning Head's tavern was just as simple as its rooms. A handful of the support beams had iron sconces attached to them, giving off little light. The air smelled of alcohol and roasted meat. And the reason Gunvald chose The Cunning Head in the first place, there were about eight other customers in the tavern. The less people who knew they were there, the better.

Gunvald and his men were seated in the corner of the room across from the front door. The same table that Gunvald had sat at six months ago when he first met Ceres...

CHAPTER SEVENTEEN
CITY OF DRIFTMOOR
SIX MONTHS EARLIER

It was six months ago when Gunvald had last been in Driftmoor. It was hot and muggy, and the whole city smelled like ass and Gunvald was sweating his balls off. If it hadn't been the only place he could find decent quality armor repair, he would never have set foot there.

It wasn't the people themselves that annoyed Gunvald; it was the sheer number of them. The market street was packed with families, children, guards, and other nuisances. Ever since Amaya killed Egil and

Leanna, Gunvald kept as far away from people as he could, unless he was killing them. The sight of other families brought back memories he didn't want to relive.

On this day, there were four guards at every corner, which could only mean one thing—someone from the royal family was out and about.

Gunvald didn't give a rat's ass about the royal family, but more guards made more congestion in the streets, which made his exit from the city that much longer.

"Leave him alone!" a young girl yelled from the alley to his left.

He knew he should have just kept walking, but a young blond girl, dressed too warmly for the heat, was yelling at a couple of older boys. Between them, a small brown dog lay on the ground, whimpering.

The boys were taking turns kicking the dog; the young girl was yelling for them to stop.

It wasn't Gunvald's business. He should have let it be. But kicking a whimpering dog? "Hey!"

The boys took one look at him, at his swords dragging behind him, and bolted down the other end of the alley. The girl stayed crying. The dog had stopped whimpering.

"He's dead," Gunvald told her.

The girl ignored him and kept crying.

Gunvald had spent a lot of time learning how not to see the spirits of the dead. It was distracting. But for whatever reason, he let his walls down.

The dog's spirit was sniffing around its dead body. Animal spirits can find their own way to the afterlife without a spirit collector, but it takes them a while.

Gunvald gently touched the girl's shoulder.

The girl pulled away. "He's not dead!"

"He's dead."

"No!" The girl put her hands on the dog's side. "I can wake him up."

There was a shift in the air. An unnatural breeze, not caused by the weather. A feeling Gunvald had only felt once before, from Amaya.

The dog's spirit cocked its head to the side. Its legs suddenly flew out from under it, and the spirit was violently dragged back into its body. The dog began whimpering again.

Gunvald stared at the girl. "What did you do?"

"I woke him up."

"No, you didn't."

The dog's spirit may have been reattached to its

body, but whatever magic the girl used did nothing to fix his injuries. Gunvald called Cinis into his hand and drove the blade into the dog's head.

The girl screamed.

Gunvald knelt beside her. "Listen to me." He grabbed her shoulders and turned her to face him.

"Listen to me. What you did just now was wrong. His body was broken. All you did was put him back into a broken body. You didn't fix him. You didn't wake him up. All you did was make him suffer more than he had to."

The girl shook her head and screeched, "And you made him better?"

"Damn it, listen, girl. No, I didn't make him better. I let him rest." Gunvald took a deep breath. "What's your name?"

The girl hesitated before answering. "Ceres."

"Listen, Ceres, whatever magic you have, it's..." Gunvald wasn't really sure what it was. "It's not something you should be using without training. And if the wrong people find out about it, it could get you into a lot of trouble."

Specifically Amaya. She would give anything to have the power to reattach spirits for her fucked-up torture hobby. The more you torture a spirit, the faster it fades away to nothing. Putting a spirit back into a body before it faded away, and extracting it whole again would give her unending joy, and Gunvald was not about to let that happen.

Ceres looked at her hands. "After I train, I can wake him up?" She looked at the dog's body.

"No!" Gunvald yelled.

Tears welled up in Ceres's eyes.

This girl was the one to make Amaya show her face. He just needed to keep her hidden from Amaya until he could figure out a plan. He called Obitus to his hand and held it to the girl's throat. "If you use your magic again, I will find out, and I will kill you. Do you understand?"

He didn't like threatening the girl, but he couldn't think of any other way to get his point across.

Ceres wiped her cheeks with the backs of her hands. "Yes."

"Good. Now–"

"There she is!" a voice yelled from the corner of the alley. Three guards were rushing towards him.

"Shit."

"You there," one guard yelled out. "Get away from the girl."

Gunvald dropped Obitus and put his hands up.

He took a few steps back. "Some boys were giving her a hard time. I was just trying to help."

Two of the guards rushed past the girl and got right in Gunvald's face. The third grabbed the girl's arm and said, "You can't wander off like that. Your father would have my head."

Gunvald couldn't hear the rest, but he heard enough to put two and two together.

He backed away, his hands still in the air. "Like I said, I was just helping the kid out."

"He was," the girl mumbled.

Gunvald turned and walked out of the alley. The guards didn't follow.

Had the dog really been dead? It had to be. He saw its spirit. The girl reattached it to its body. Gunvald didn't think that was possible. If it was, Amaya would have been using it for her little torture games. A forgotten magic, perhaps? Gunvald didn't know enough to be sure. He knew one thing, though.

Amaya would want that power for herself. And she would come out of hiding to get it.

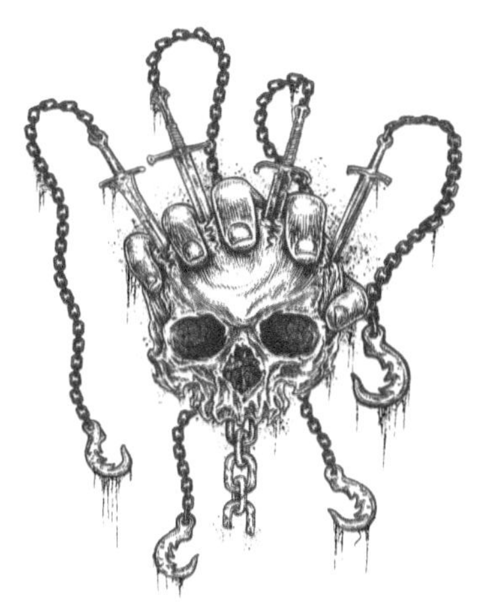

CHAPTER EIGHTEEN
DRIFTMOOR SEWERS

"Oh, come on," Darius moaned. "Are you fucking serious?"

The moon dipped in and out of the clouds, but gave off just enough light to see the stream from the sewer outlet. The tunnel stunk of shit and piss, and excrement was floating freely. The people in the castle must be eating well tonight.

"Is it too late to pick a different way in?" Darius asked.

Bear rested his giant mallet on his shoulder and stepped into the stream. "Yes, now stop whining and get in here."

"Ugh," Darius stepped into the stream and gagged. "I can't do it."

"Suck it up," Gunvald said.

The swords began whispering in his head again, but it wasn't bloodlust this time. Evidently, being dragged through shit and piss wasn't in their job description. Not that Gunvald cared, but he kind of preferred the bloodlust to their disgusted whining.

About thirty feet in from the tunnel exit, they were in complete darkness.

"A little light?" Gunvald said.

Gunvald could hear Darius mutter, and then a small orb of light appeared in Darius's hand.

The sewer tunnels were big enough for them to stand straight up, but so narrow they had to walk single file. Thankfully, the sewage was only ankle-deep.

Darius retched and gagged until he finally vomited.

"Control yourself, D," Bear said.

"Shut the fuck up."

"I will gladly help you with your gag reflex, if you want."

"Seriously, shut it."

Bear laughed. "I'm just saying."

"Enough, you two," Gunvald growled.

"Yes, Mom," Bear said.

The tunnel branched off in three directions. Gunvald paused and tried to remember which path led under the castle.

"Left," Bear said.

Gunvald walked down the left tunnel without thinking much about it. He was thinking about the swords. They had stopped their whispering for a while now, and their silence was making him anxious.

"There," Bear said, pointing to a rough patch in the smooth tunnel wall. He walked over to the patch, hauled back, and swung his giant mallet. The sound of steel hitting stone echoed through the tunnel, and chunks of stone flew in every direction.

Bear swung again, and the hole became just big enough for them to fit through. Gunvald nodded for Darius to take a look. "Looks like the tunnel's still here," he said.

"After you," Gunvald said.

Darius sighed and stepped into the tunnel. Gunvald followed with Bear bringing up the rear.

"I remember the tunnel being a little wider than this," Bear said.

The tunnel was so tight Gunvald could hear

Bear's armor scraping along the walls. "I think you're a little wider," Gunvald said.

"Maybe," Bear replied.

It was only a minute or two later that Gunvald spotted the wall leading into the prison cell over Darius's shoulder.

"I think we're here," Darius said.

"About time," Bear said, panting. "I'm dying back here."

Darius laughed. "It's all them cakes and cookies, fat boy."

"I'm gonna cake and cookie your face if you don't open that wall," Bear said.

Darius drew the mage cannon from his right holster and pointed it at the rough stone wall. Gunvald and Bear covered their ears.

BOOM!

Debris pelted Gunvald from every angle; dust filled the tunnel. Darius coughed so hard, Gunvald thought his little head might explode. The gunmage holstered the spell pistol and waved the dust from his face. "That coulda gone a little better."

Bear grunted. "At least you let them know we're here."

When the dust settled, Gunvald saw that the

hole was maybe big enough for Darius's skinny ass to fit through.

"I can't even get my arm through that." Bear said.

"Relax," Darius said. He crawled through the hole and kicked at the makeshift limestone from the other side until it was big enough for Gunvald to fit through. Bear on the other hand...

"Bunch of skinny fucks," Bear muttered as he rammed his left shoulder into the top of the hole, knocking off a large chunk of wall before stepping through.

Bear's assumption that King Adder had turned the cells back into a storage room couldn't have been more wrong. Darius's light spell illuminated the same prison cell that had been there before.

"Oh yay, a jail cell. This brings back memories," Darius muttered.

Gunvald walked over and pushed the cell door. It creaked open with a loud squeal. The room looked as if it hadn't been used since Adder took the castle. Inches of dust covered the few wooden barrels stacked up on the far side of the room next to a couple of shattered wooden boxes.

"Let's go." Gunvald stepped out of the cell and tried the door out of the cell block. "Son of a bitch."

"Locked?" Darius asked.

"I got it," Bear said.

Bear took a few steps back, charged the door, and slammed it with his shoulder. It flung open and crashed against the outside wall.

Gunvald called the long sword Dimittis to his hand and walked through. As he had hoped, the corridor was empty except for a couple of rats scratching around. At the end was an ascending stairway.

"What now?" Darius asked.

"Up the stairs to the kitchen," Gunvald said. "We'll cut through there and take the south tower stairs to the third floor. We'll figure the rest out from there."

Eventually, he'd have to come clean to Darius about his plan to lure out Amaya, but he hoped to find Adder's daughter first.

"I'll go check it out." Darius dimmed his light spell and crept to the staircase.

When Darius was out of earshot, Gunvald asked Bear, "You sure you're good with this?"

"Doesn't matter. We're here. Let's just get it done with."

Darius whistled from the darkness—the all clear, which was surprising. During Gunvald's time at the castle, there were always some staff in the kitchen. Gunvald released Dimittis, and all four swords retracted and slipped under his cloak against his back. He hated having them this close to him.

"Let's go."

Darius's light spell led Gunvald and Bear to the stairs.

"Okay, cut the light," Gunvald said halfway up the staircase. "The door at the far end of the kitchen leads to a small alcove. The south stairs are on the right. There's an archway on the left. Watch for guards there."

"Got it," Darius said. The light winked out.

They continued up toward the kitchen. Halfway up, they heard a loud metallic clang. Gunvald looked at Darius.

Darius shrugged. "What? It was clear a second ago," he whispered.

Gunvald shook his head. He waved Darius to lead the way to the top of the stairs. Darius sighed and crept past him. He stopped near the top of the stairs and peeked around the corner. He held his hand up and then waved them to follow.

There were two torches lit in the kitchen. A half-cleaned-up puddle of water lay to the left of the door they needed to get to. Gunvald hurried across and pressed his back against the right of the door. Darius and Bear followed and pressed themselves to the left.

They heard footsteps approaching from the other side of the door and Gunvald cursed to himself. The door swung open, almost crushing Darius and Bear behind it. A servant woman entered the kitchen with a mop in hand.

Gunvald grabbed her around the neck with his left arm and clamped his right hand over her mouth. She dropped her mop and clawed his arms. Darius caught the mop before it hit the floor.

Gunvald choked the air out of her, trying not to kill her. When she went limp, he dragged her across the kitchen and gently set her down on the staircase. Darius glared at him as he walked back to the door.

"Gun, for fuck's sake—"

"Relax, she's still alive." Gunvald waved Darius through the door. "Get going."

Darius headed down the dark corridor, Gunvald and Bear behind him. He pointed to the staircase to the right of a small alcove. Gunvald nodded.

They crept up the stairs, past the second-floor alcove, which was empty, and up to the third.

There was one closed door, an unlit chandelier, and a murder hole leaking moonlight on the landing.

"What now?" Darius whispered.

"We cut through there," Gunvald said, nodding towards a door that led to a communal room where guards took their breaks. Gunvald had been up there a few times when he was working guard duty for King Ranton.

Bear looked at him like he thought he was missing something. "There'll probably be guards."

"Then we deal with them. It's the only way."

"How many?" Darius asked.

"A few at least," Bear said.

"I got this," Darius said, drawing out a mage cannon. "I stored some spells specifically for this situation."

Gunvald's swords started whispering in his head again.

Blood! It's been too long!

Despite it's annoyance, Gunvald liked it much better than their anxious silence.

Darius crept up to the communal room door, pressed his ear against it, and after a few seconds held up three fingers. Then he waggled his hand and held up four.

Gunvald called Dimittis to his hand. Darius grabbed the door handle and yanked it open.

AMAYA

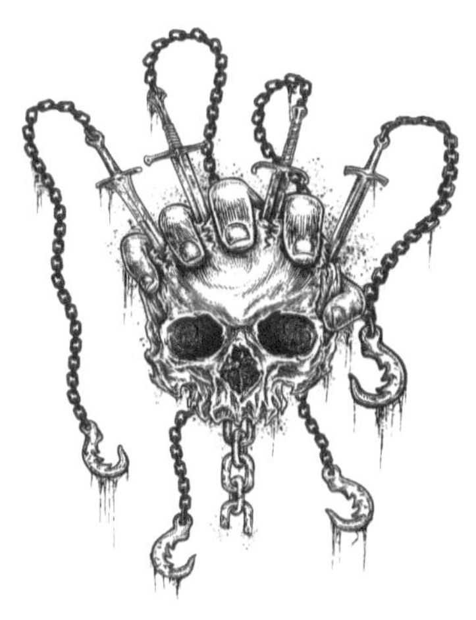

CHAPTER NINETEEN
DRIFTMOOR CASTLE

Three guards were seated at a small table; a fourth was leaning against the wall on the right.

Darius shot two spell bullets at the two guards at the table. One fell backwards to the floor. The other slumped forward and slammed his head on the table. Darius switched the cannon to his right hand and shot another two spell bullets at the other two guards. Both collapsed to the floor. Darius spun his cannon and shoved it back into his holster.

A fifth guard had been standing by a door in the corner. The man reached for his sword. Gunvald ran over and plunged Dimittis through the guard's neck. Blood gushed over Gunvald's hand and arm. He yanked out the longsword and let the guard's body fall to the ground.

Bear shook his head at Darius. "You missed one."

"Shut up," Darius asked. "And you know I just put mine to sleep, right?"

Gunvald shrugged, stepped forward, and almost fell over. The swords hissed into his head.

Stupid gunmage! Stupid!

"Hey, are you okay?" Darius asked him.

Gunvald held his hand out. "Stay away."

Kill him! Let us kill him!

Gunvald clenched his teeth. "I'm not fucking killing him."

"Gunvald?" Bear asked.

Gunvald shook his head. "It's nothing."

Gunvald took a deep breath. The whispering faded away. "I'm fine."

"You don't look fine," Darius said.

Gunvald wiped the sweat from his forehead with his forearm. "You a healer?"

Darius glanced at Bear, and Bear shrugged.

"Okay, then," Gunvald said, straightening up

and grimacing. "Let's go."

"Where are we going exactly?" Darius asked.

"Bear will head to the west side stairs and check the fourth floor library. We'll go east and hit the king's study."

Bear said nothing. He gave Gunvald a long, cold look and nodded. "Fine."

"The king's study?" Darius said. "I've always wanted to see one."

Gunvald pushed the door open and stepped out into the hallway. Darius followed him while Bear went in the opposite direction.

Halfway down the hallway, Darius whispered, "You sure splitting up's a good idea?"

"Bear probably knows this castle better than most of the people that live here. He'll be fine."

"Yeah, but what about us?" Darius asked.

"Don't worry so much."

Gunvald couldn't take his own advice. He was nervous. The only reason he sent Bear on his own was to find Ceres. Heading to the king's study was just another way to keep Darius in the dark.

They slunk down the hallway and stopped near the eastern stairs. Someone was coming down. Light footsteps, no armor clinking. Most likely, a servant.

Gunvald and Darius pressed themselves up against the wall. A servant woman descended the stairway and continued down the hallway in front of them, seemingly oblivious to their presence.

Gunvald nodded, and he and Darius hurried up the stairs.

Gunvald peered out from the top of the stairs into the fourth-floor hallway. No guards, no servants. He stepped into the hallway and pressed himself against the wall. Darius did the same behind him. The king's study was only four doors down, but it seemed like miles.

Soon he was going to have to tell Darius that the real reason they were here was to kill the king's daughter. Darius would never hurt a child. Even if the child killed his whole family, it's a line Darius would never cross.

It was the one thing they all said they would never do, and yet here he was, planning to do just that. Gunvald had no doubt he would be dead before the night was over; either Amaya would peel his flesh from his bones, or Darius would shoot him.

He just hoped if it was the latter, Darius would at least do it after they killed Amaya. The closer they got to the king's study, the more Gunvald was starting to regret the plan, but they were already too far into it to stop.

As they approached the door of the study, Darius crept up and pressed his ear against it, listened a few seconds, and shook his head. "Somebody's moving around in there."

Gunvald cursed under his breath.

The only people he'd seen spend any time in the study while he was at the castle were King Ranton and his family. So it'd be fair to say that Adder would be the same way. If it was Adder inside, having Darius put him to sleep might actually be helpful.

"If Adder's in there, just put him to sleep," Gunvald whispered.

Darius nodded. "Got it."

Darius pushed the door open and rushed inside the study. Sure enough, King Adder was sitting at his desk on the right side of the room, reading. Darius raised his pistol and shot him in the neck with a sleep bullet.

Adder dropped the book on the floor, slumped forward, and smacked his head on the desk.

"Oh, shit," Darius said as Adder's daughter stood up from behind the desk.

What the hell was she doing up so late?

"Daddy?" She shook Adder's shoulder. "Daddy, wake up."

Darius cleared his throat. "Don't worry, he's fine. He's just sleeping."

"Ceres, do you remember me? We met in the alley a few months ago?"

Ceres looked at Gunvald and nodded.

"Good. Look, we're not here to hurt anyone—"

Ceres ran for a side door, pulled it open, and ran straight into Bear.

Bear grabbed the girl and clamped his free hand over her mouth.

"Bear?! What the fuck?" Darius asked.

Bear said nothing. He just stared at Gunvald. Ceres kicked and struggled but Bear held her tight. Eventually she gave up struggling, most likely realizing there was no escaping Bear's grasp.

Kill her! Kill him! Blood! Kill them all!

Gunvald clenched his teeth and walked toward Bear and Ceres.

"You okay, Gun?" Darius asked.

Blood!

"Gunvald!"

He wanted it. Needed it.

"Gun, stop!" Darius's voice sounded miles away.

Gunvald took another step forward. Kill the girl and Amaya will show. Then he could kill Amaya. Then Bear, and Darius, and Adder, and anyone else that got in his way.

"Gunvald, get any closer, and I swear I'll drop you."

Gunvald stopped. The whispers stopped. Gunvald realized he was gripping Cinis so hard his knuckles were white. Ceres's eyes were wide, staring at him.

Darius lowered the pistol, looked at Gunvald, then at Bear. "Somebody tell me what the fuck is going on, cause it looks like you were about to kill the kid."

It was not how things were supposed to go, and it was time to let Darius know.

CHAPTER TWENTY
THE KING'S STUDY

"I lied about not knowing who the necromancer was." Gunvald pointed Cinis at Ceres. "She's the necromancer."

Darius gaped at him. "What do you mean, she's the necromancer?"

Gunvald sighed. "She can reattach spirits."

"So you were gonna kill her?"

Bear shifted his weight, and Darius drew his other mage cannon and aimed it at him. "Bear, I swear to every god imaginable, if you move a single muscle, I will put a hole in your head."

Gunvald sighed. "Listen, Darius—"

"What, girl killer?" Darius said. "I'm listening."

"It's the only way."

Darius raised the pistol toward Gunvald's face. "No, it isn't, Gunvald. We don't kill kids."

Blood! Kill them! Kill the girl! She's so sweet!

Gunvald clenched his eyes shut, but it didn't help, so he opened them again. "It's not that simple."

"The fuck it isn't. What was the plan? The actual plan. Kill the kid to piss off Amaya? Hope she comes to kill us and kill her instead?"

Gunvald shrugged.

Stab him! Let me do it!

"Are you fucking serious? That's the most asinine thing I've ever heard. If you had told me, I would have saved us the fucking trouble of coming here."

"If I had told you, you wouldn't have gone through with it."

"Damn fucking right, and I'd be telling you the same shit I am now, but at least we'd be in some shithole tavern instead of the goddamned king's study."

Kill him! Now!

Gunvald shook his head. "No."

Darius stared at him. "No, what?"

"I need this, Darius," Gunvald said. "Amaya needs to pay for what she's done. She needs to die."

"No shit," Darius said, waggling the pistol at him. "But this is not the fucking way to do it."

"Don't you think I've tried every other way? Killed every goddamn high-profile noble, warlord, peasant and slaver I could to lure her out?"

Gunvald pointed Cinis at Darius. "This is it. She is it. This is how we get Amaya."

"I won't let you kill an innocent kid to make that happen."

"Then what do we do? Kidnap her? The king's men will hunt us for the rest of our lives." Gunvald looked at the girl for the first time in several minutes. She was a cute kid. Messy blond hair. Fancy nightshirt. She seemed to be watching them with quite a bit of interest, or was that fear? Darius was right—it was sad she had to die.

The whispers in his head stopped. "Well, we sure as shit can't just leave her here now. As soon as her powers awaken, Amaya will be all over her, using her to endlessly torture spirits. I will not give her that pleasure!"

"Don't even fucking go there, Gunvald, because I swear I will put a bullet right between your fucking eyes."

The swords started up again.

Kill him. He has ruined everything!

Gunvald wanted nothing more than to stab Darius in the throat.

"Maybe he's right, Gunvald," Bear said. "Maybe we should just give it up."

"No!" Gunvald yelled. "This is what we came here to do! Don't you fucking back out now!"

Kill the big one! Kill him!

Obitus slithered into Gunvald's free hand, almost startling Gunvald.

"Listen to yourself, Gunvald," Darius said. "This isn't you."

"Bear!" Gunvald yelled.

With a reluctant look on his face, Bear moved his arm from across Ceres's stomach up towards her neck.

Darius pointed the gun at Bear's face. "Don't fucking move, Bear. Don't you fucking move!" He snapped the spell ring on the gun into position.

Gunvald stared at him and tightened his grip on his swords.

Kill them both! Now! You must!

Gunvald could feel himself giving in.

"Don't listen to them, Gunvald," Darius said. "Whatever those fucking swords are saying, don't listen."

Ceres shook her head out of Bear's grasp. "Please don't kill me," she said, tears welling up in her eyes.

Visions of Egil flashed in Gunvald's head, practicing his sword, brushing the horse, listening to Gunvald's monster stories in bed. Now Gunvald had become one of those monsters.

Kill the girl! Kill the gunmage...

"Fuck off! No."

Gunvald dropped the swords.

"Thank the fucking gods," Darius said.

Dimittis sprang up and plunged itself through Ceres's neck and into Bear's stomach. They fell to the floor.

"No!" Darius ran over and knelt next to Bear and Ceres. Gunvald stepped toward them, but Darius whipped his mage cannon around and pointed it at his face.

"Don't even," Darius snarled. "Just stay the fuck over there."

Gunvald stepped back to the door they'd entered from. "I didn't do it, Darius. It wasn't me."

"You or the swords, it doesn't matter. Just don't

fucking move!"

Bear groaned, clutching his stomach, blood seeping through his fingers. Ceres was already dead, face down on the floor in a puddle of her own blood.

Darius cursed and patted Bear on the shoulder. "Just hang in there, Bear."

Bear pulled himself to a sitting position and leaned against the door frame. "I'm done for D."

Gunvald shook his head. "No, you're not."

"It's fine," Bear closed his eyes.

"No, it's fucking not," Darius said. "It's not fine. None of this is fine. The girl's dead, you're dying, he's out of control, and we're completely fucked."

Bear leaned his head against the door frame. "What's done... is done."

Gunvald watched them from the door near the hallway. He wanted to help, but he didn't want to get his head blown off... or maybe he did. He took a step forward. "It wasn't me, Darius. The swords..."

"Just shut the fuck up, Gun." Darius glared at him.

"D, do me... one last favor," Bear said. He took his hand off his belly. Blood and viscera glopped out onto the dead girl.

"What?"

"How about... a kiss goodbye?"

"Oh, fuck you, man," Darius said.

Bear laughed until he choked on his blood and dribbled it down his chin. "It was worth... a shot..."

"Don't fucking die, Bear. We're gonna get outta this shit."

"Just do me one thing, D." Bear wretched on his blood. "Make sure... that bitch... joins me in Helios."

Darius looked up and scrambled back to the center of the room.

"How touching," Amaya said, stepping over Ceres and into the study. She knelt down and placed her hand on the girl's head. "Such a waste."

She was there for the girl's birthday or for her death. Either way, Gunvald was right.

He glared at her and stepped forward. "You fucking b—"

Amaya barely glanced at him.

"Hello, Gunvald, give me a minute." She leaned down and whispered in the dead girl's ear. Ceres's spirit rose from her body. She was crying. Amaya smoothed the spirit girl's hair. "Don't worry, Ceres. You will enjoy Astrum." Then the spirit vanished as if it had never been there.

Amaya stood up and turned to Gunvald.

"I'll be honest with you, Gunvald. You surprise me. I didn't think you'd kill a child to get my attention."

"I didn't—" Gunvald lowered his head. He knew the girl would still be alive if not for his desire for revenge on Amaya, swords or no swords. "I didn't kill her. The swords..."

"Oh, but you did," Amaya said. "Do you still not understand the weapons I gave you?"

Gunvald stared at her, fists clenched. The swords started whispering.

Kill her. Don't be afraid. Do it!

He shook his head. "I didn't kill them."

"You still fail to understand, my dear," Amaya said. "The swords cannot act on their own. They react to your feelings, your thoughts, thoughts that are so far in the back of your mind you don't even know you're thinking them. So, yes, Gunvald. You killed them."

She was wrong. She was just trying to get in his head. How could she know what they could do? She couldn't even touch the damned things after they attached themselves to him.

"I didn't tell them to kill the girl! I tried to stop them."

"No, Gunvald, you didn't. You've been using

the power I granted you to suffocate them. To prevent them from accessing the deepest parts of your mind, but with that power gone, they act upon your genuine desires."

"I didn't desire to kill her... or Bear! Why would I kill my friend?" Gunvald called Cinis to his hand.

Amaya shrugged. "Perhaps... perhaps not."

Gunvald charged and swung Cinis at her throat. Amaya caught the blade in her right hand, and punched her left palm into Gunvald's sternum, sending him flying backwards across the floor into the bookshelves. The entire top shelf of books tumbled down onto his head.

Amaya shook her head. "You've killed a lot of people to get my attention, Gunvald. Do you know why I never showed up? It wasn't that the people weren't important enough..."

She lies! Kill her now!

"I don't care anymore," Gunvald growled.

Gunvald charged again and swung Cinis at her head. An elegant, black rapier materialized in her hand, and she blocked the blow. Gunvald swung again; Amaya deflected it and gashed Gunvald's right arm.

Gunvald stepped back and grabbed his arm.

Darius fired the mage cannon at Amaya. A

flame-spell bullet burned away a chunk of her arm.

Amaya laughed. She vanished and instantly reappeared next to Darius. "That's a nasty little toy you have there, Darius." She tried to stick him in the neck with the point of her rapier, but Obitus shot out and deflected the blade. Gunvald swung Cinis with both hands at Amaya's head.

Amaya blocked the wide blade with her hand and sliced Gunvald's other arm. Gunvald thrust his sword at her chest, but she disappeared.

"Tsk, tsk, tsk," she said from across the room. The arm that Darius burned had already healed. "You've become slow and predictable, Gunvald."

Darius jumped up and stood next to Gunvald. Both men clutched their weapons with white knuckles.

"I didn't want it to go this way, Gunvald," Amaya said. "I had hoped you'd give up after a while when I didn't show up. Run away to some small town and live the rest of your life in peace."

"Fuck off," Gunvald said.

"If you had stopped, I was more than willing to forget everything." Amaya smiled. "Despite what you might think, I do care for you, Gunvald. If you had just stopped and lived out your life, I would have eventually sent you and your family to Astrum."

"Eventually?! What the fuck does that mean?!"

"I'm sorry, Gunvald. They deserved to go to Astrum; they really did. But you angered me so with your arrogance."

"What. Did. You. Do. To. Them?"

Amaya turned her head away and sighed. "The Ashlands, Gunvald. I sent them to the Ashlands. I'm sorry, Gunvald."

"You're not sorry. You're fucking dead."

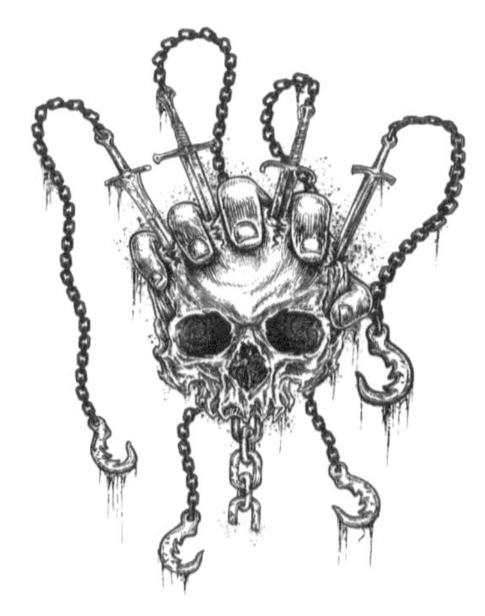

CHAPTER TWENTY-ONE
THE KING'S STUDY

Gunvald called Iudicium to his hand and sliced horizontally at Amaya's throat with all his might. Amaya raised her rapier to block, and Obitus shot forward at her chest. Amaya whipped her sword around and swatted Obitus away.

Darius shot her in the shoulder. A chunk of ice encased her upper arm, and Gunvald slashed Amaya across the stomach. Amaya pulled her arm down, breaking the ice, and backhanded Gunvald in his face, sending him tumbling backward.

Darius shot another spell bullet at Amaya's

wrist, and another at her leg. Ice crackled over both wounds.

Gunvald dropped Iudicium, called Cinis back into his hand, and swung its massive blade at her chest. Amaya blocked the blade with the ice on her wrist, showering both of them with ice shards.

Gunvald kicked her leg, and she stumbled against the king's desk. Obitus rose from the floor and thrust itself into her gut. Gunvald swung again for her neck. She raised her rapier and blocked the blow, but the sword spun out of her hand.

Amaya stepped around the desk, clutching her gut. Blood blotted her black dress. Darius hit her shoulder with a spell bullet. Her shoulder sizzled, and the smell of burned flesh wafted into the air, and then the wound closed, just like all the others. Even the burn on her dress disappeared.

"Enough!" She thrust out her left arm; a giant hand of smoke shot out, wrapped itself around Darius, and threw him backwards into the bookshelves. He slammed his head and crumpled to the floor.

Gunvald tried to rush her, but she thrust her hand out and sent him tumbling across the floor.

"You wanted my attention, Gunvald? You wanted to get your revenge?" Ashen-colored smoke slithered up Amaya's arms, around her body, and over her face. Her skin pulled taunt, revealing every skeletal feature. Her eyes became hollow voids. Her dress transformed into a ragged black robe. Black chains, like the ones on Gunvald's swords, writhed and coiled around her body and hung from her billowing sleeves. A black, smoking scythe formed in her hand. "Well, here I am, Gunvald. Come and get me."

Gunvald got to his feet and gripped Cinis with both hands.

Kill her! Do not be afraid!

He stepped forward carefully, Cinis out in front of his chest and face.

Amaya feinted a slice at Gunvald's crotch and sliced Gunvald across his chest with her scythe, spraying blood into the air as her blade cut through his cuirass as if it wasn't even there.

Gunvald thrust Cinis at Amaya's chest. She blocked it easily with the haft of her scythe, caught the blade, and threw it clattering against a side table by the window. Then sliced Gunvald's arm, leaving a flap of blood-dripping skin hanging off it.

Dimittis rose from the floor on its own and flew at Amaya's chest, but she swatted it away and slammed Gunvald in the face with the handle of her scythe. A tooth flew out of his mouth, and he stumbled into a reading chair, drooling blood over its fine upholstery. Then she grabbed him by the neck, lifted him up, and slammed him face first into the wooden floor.

Gunvald slowly pushed himself up to his knees and stared up at Amaya, broken nose, blood dripping into his eye from his forehead. She stared down at him and him and laughed. "Are we done yet?"

Gunvald tried to get up, but his body wouldn't listen. The swords screamed in his head.

We will not die here! Death must die! Kill her! Let us! We will give you the power!

Gunvald knew what they wanted. They wanted to take over. They wanted to enslave him.

There would be no more Gunvald, just a puppet of a bloodthirsty magic. They would use his body to slaughter everyone in the castle. But they might be able to kill Amaya, and right now, that was all that mattered.

"Fine," he whispered. "Just do it."

"Oh, sweetie," Amaya said. "I don't need your permission to kill you."

Gunvald chuckled. "I wasn't talking to you."

One after the other, Dimittis, Iudicium, Cinis, and Obitus rose from the floor and plunged themselves into Gunvald's back. Oily, red and black vines crawled out of each wound, slithered into his hands, and grew into a curved, black sword.

He smelled a faint scent of decay pouring off of it. He felt his hand clutch the hilt so hard he thought he might crush it between his fingers. His chest filled with power. He looked at the black blade, and it spoke to him.

Now you have become Death. She will fall!

When he stood up, the other four swords fell out of him and clattered to the floor. Gunvald rushed at Amaya and swung his sword down, hoping to split Amaya's head in half, but Amaya blocked the blade with her scythe. Gunvald brought the blade around and sliced it across Amaya's chest.

Amaya gasped and clutched her chest. Ashen smoke puffed from the wound, and blood spilled down her ragged black robe. She pressed the two edges of the cut together, but the wound split open again and more blood seeped into her robe. She gaped at Gunvald, eyes wide, mouth hanging open.

Yes! She bleeds! Finish her!

With one hand on her chest and the other gripping the haft of her scythe, Amaya swung the blade at Gunvald's knees. Gunvald jumped back just in time. He lunged forward and swung at Amaya's side. She twirled the scythe around and blocked it with the haft. Then she spun around and sliced Gunvald across the back. Gunvald could feel the blood sticking to his under garment but he felt no pain. He swung his sword up, catching Amaya's thigh and spraying blood on both of them.

"Enough of this shit," she spat. She raised her hands in the air, scythe blade over her head, and stared down at the four bloody swords on the floor. "Come to me, my darlings!"

A black cloud appeared in the middle of the room. Gunvald stepped back, expecting the swords to turn on him, but instead they shot their chains at Amaya and wrapped around her arms and legs, digging their hooks into her flesh. She screamed.

Now! Kill her!

Gunvald lunged forward and thrust the black sword into her chest. He twisted the blade and wrenched it back out.

Blood gushed from the wound. Amaya's face went pale. She stared at him. Tears welled up in her eyes. She extended her free hand toward him.

The chains pulled her down to her knees in front of Gunvald. He raised the black sword over his head.

Kill her, you fool! Now is your chance!

"Even if you kill me," Amaya said, almost in a whisper, "your family is still in the Ashlands. Only I can free them, and you know it. Release me and—"

Gunvald plunged the sword into the top of Amaya's head. He twisted the blade and yanked it out. The four sword's chains unwound from Amaya's body and retracted into their pommels. Amaya fell face first on the floor, blood and brains spilling from the top of her head.

Gunvald stared at the body. He had done it. The black sword whispered in his mind, *Alas, I am free.*

The door to the hallway flew open.

Two guards rushed into the room, swords drawn. They looked at Gunvald and attacked. The first thrust his sword at Gunvald's chest. The black sword swung up almost before Gunvald willed it and whacked the guard's blade aside. Then it sliced across the guard's chest, cutting clean through his armor and gouging his flesh. He fell forward, bounced off a reading chair, and toppled to the floor.

The other guard charged. Gunvald steadied himself and raised the black sword in front of him. Then... BANG... a bloody hole erupted in the man's face.

Darius crawled to one knee. "There we go."

"It's about fucking time you got up."

Darius laughed. "You're welcome."

Blood. Kill him. Kill the gunmage!

Gunvald turned and stared at Darius.

"No! Leave him alone!" He stepped toward Darius and raised the black blade.

Darius stepped toward the door. "It's those fucking swords, isn't it? Stay away from me!" He raised his mage cannon and pointed it at Gunvald.

Do it! Feed us his blood.

Gunvald's body took another step forward.

Darius's gun hand trembled. "Come on, man. Don't make me kill you."

Gunvald wasn't in control anymore. He stepped over Amaya's body toward Darius. Then he stopped. He could feel his body wanting to move, but something was holding him in place.

Let us go! We must kill the gunmage!

"Well, this is quite the scene," a woman's voice said behind him.

"Who the hell are you?" Darius asked.

"Let's get these out of your head, shall we?" she said.

No! Vile woman!

She waved her hand, and the black sword in Gunvald's hand was gone, as were the swords voices. Gunvald had gotten so used to having them in his head that the silence was unnerving.

The woman was just a little taller than Amaya. Her shoulder-length black hair had bright red streaks that seemed to flicker like flames, and her leather dress looked like flowing black armor.

"Who are you?" Darius asked again, pointing his mage cannon at the woman.

The woman smiled, walked across the room, and looked down at Amaya's body. "You can't keep swearing to the gods and not expect one to eventually show up." The woman turned to Darius and curtsied. "Velena, Queen of Helios... at your service."

CHAPTER TWENTY-TWO
THE KING'S STUDY

Velena stared down at Amaya's body, shook her head and tsked. "Such a shame it had to come to this." Then she turned and walked over to Gunvald, who was still frozen in place. "So this is the man she was so enamored with?" She placed a finger under Gunvald's chin and raised his face. "You do have a sort of rugged charm to you." She took her hand away.

"What do you want?" Darius asked.

"What indeed?" Velena placed her hands on her hips. "It seems I am in need of a new Death." She looked Gunvald up and down again.

Darius pointed the mage cannon at her head.

"I won't let you take him." The spell ring clicked into place.

Velena smirked.

Gunvald looked sideways at Darius. "Run," he said weakly.

"You should listen to your friend," Velena said. "I have no quarrel with you at the moment, but keep pointing that thing in my face..."

Darius's jaw clenched, and his lips tightened. He lowered his mage cannon and arched his brow at Gunvald.

"It's fine." Gunvald told him. "Just go."

Darius stared at him for a moment, then at Velena. "What about his family? That bitch sent them to the Ashlands for no fucking reason. They didn't deserve that."

"Maybe, maybe not," Velena said. "It will be sorted out in time."

"That's not good enough," Darius raised the cannon again.

Gunvald whispered, "Darius, put it down."

Velena seemed to pay no attention to the mage cannon pointed at her face. She stared at Gunvald. "If you be a good little Death, maybe I'll let you send your family where they belong."

"Don't do it, Gun," Darius said. "Let me blow her to pieces."

Velena smiled at Gunvald. "Your friend's about to get himself killed."

"Darius... just leave," Gunvald said.

"Fuck," Darius shook his head and holstered the mage cannon. "At least send Bear to Astrum. He deserves that much."

Gunvald looked at Bear's body. Bear's spirit was standing next to it. He looked content.

Velena waved her hand at Bear's corpse in the doorway. "Done."

Gunvald watched as Bear's spirit rose and disappeared in a bright white light.

Darius looked at Gunvald, who nodded.

"Now, you had best be going," Velena said. She waved her hand, and Darius disappeared. "He was getting on my nerves."

"What did...?" Gunvald asked.

"He'll be fine," Velena said. "A little nauseous perhaps." She placed her hand on Gunvald's shoulder. "Come now, Gunvald. I've spent more than enough time on this plane. It's time to go home."

Gunvald wanted to protest, but he was losing a

lot of blood. He was having trouble staying conscious, never mind speaking.

Velena waved her hand, and a black, inky circle appeared beneath Gunvald. Skeletal hands shot up from the darkness, grabbed onto his legs, and dragged him down into the darkness.

* * *

SEVEN MONTHS LATER

It was too damned hot. The air, the ground, the horse Gunvald was riding, all of it. He rode from one dead body to a whole slew of them, to a town of them, to a battlefield of them, sending the dead where they needed to go. But he was not Death. He couldn't vanish and reappear wherever he wanted. He had half of a grim-form, and worst of all, he was still burdened with the fucking swords. At least now he could control them, but their constant whispering was getting on his last nerve.

His steed, if you could call it that, was a skeleton of a horse with thin skin stretched taut over its bones. It never neighed, snorted, drank, ate, or even tired, and he was chained to the damned thing.

One end was wrapped around the beast's neck and the other to Gunvald's leg. They didn't restrict his movement. He couldn't feel them, but he could see them. Flickering in a pale blue light. They only let him get so far from the beast before pulling him back.

The Deldosa Plains were as dusty as they were barren. Gunvald rode most of the way there with his arm in front of his face in a futile attempt to keep the dust from his eyes.

An old man's body lay by the side of the road. Short gray hair, a stubbled beard, torso half-eaten by crows. His spirit was stumbling around near his body, shimmering faint blue. He was destined for Astrum.

Gunvald dismounted and walked to it.

"Sorry for the wait." He'd been saying that a lot lately.

"Oh my," the old man's spirit said. "Is it my time already?"

Gunvald nodded. "It is."

"That's too bad." The man frowned. "I was hoping to see my daughter one last time."

"Is that where you were heading?" Gunvald asked.

"I-I don't really remember."

Gunvald sighed. The longer a spirit waited to be

sent to the afterlife, the more it forgot its previous life. The more it forgot who it was. Not that Gunvald particularly cared. The only thing that mattered was getting his family out of the Ashlands.

Gunvald put his hand on the spirit's shoulder. "It's time to go."

"Thank you, son." The old man's spirit rippled. Then his face contorted. He let out a scream and grabbed his head with both hands. "What are you—"

Gunvald removed his hand from the old man's shoulder. A bright white light engulfed the old man's spirit, and it vanished.

Gunvald trudged back over to his beast. He called Dimittis to his hand and stabbed the horse straight through the chest. It let out a raspy neigh and crumbled to the ground.

"Fuck!"

Gunvald threw Dimittis onto the dusty ground.

He didn't have the power to enter the Ashlands on his own, but that didn't mean it was impossible. And just like the last time he tried, he couldn't send anyone to the Ashlands.

The horse grunted and then stood back up.

Gunvald sighed. He had killed the beast more times than he could count, trying to free himself of his chains, and would no doubt kill it many more times. He would find a way to unchain himself from the wretched creature.

Gunvald climbed back in the saddle and groaned. His body ached. If he abandoned his duties as Death for too long, his body would become wracked with pain. But that didn't stop him from trying.

The horse started walking. Like the horse, Gunvald could also sense the spirits of the dead, but he was content to let the beast take him wherever it wanted to go, and it always took him to the nearest waiting spirit. But there will be a day when he walks the fucking beast into the Ashlands and frees his family. And not Velena, or any other god, will stop him.

ABOUT THE AUTHOR

Michael Doyle is the award winning author of the fast-paced, middle-grade fantasy adventure series James's Ragtag Adventures in Questworld. A cable installer by trade, Michael has been writing horror and fantasy stories for a little over 30 years, and pursuing it professionally for the past 5 years. When he isn't writing, Michael can be found playing video games, adding unneeded toys to his toy collection, or helping his daughter write her own books and run her Youtube channel.

www.mdoylebooks.com
facebook.com/mdoylebhp
instagram.com/mdoylebhp
tiktok.com/@mdoylebooks
youtube.com/@mdoylebhp
bsky.app/profile/mdoylebhp.bsky.social